Cubana

edited by
M i r t a **Y** á ñ e z

foreword by
R u t h **B** e h a r

translated by
D i c k **C** l u s t e r a n d
C i n d y **S** c h u s t e r

Cubana

Contemporary Fiction by Cuban Women

Beacon Press
Boston

BEACON PRESS
25 Beacon Street
Boston, Massachusetts 02108-2892
www.beacon.org

BEACON PRESS BOOKS
are published under the auspices of
the Unitarian Universalist Association of Congregations.

03 02 01 00 99 98   8 7 6 5 4 3 2 1

This book is printed on recycled acid-free paper that contains
at least 20 percent postconsumer waste and meets the uncoated paper ANSI/NISO
specifications for permanence as revised in 1992.

Text design by Anne Chalmers
Composition by Wilsted & Taylor Publishing Services

Library of Congress Cataloging-in-Publication Data

Cubana : contemporary fiction by Cuban women / edited by Mirta Yáñez ;
foreword by Ruth Behar ; translated by Dick Cluster and Cindy Schuster.
      p. cm.
ISBN 0-8070-8336-4 (cloth : alk. paper). —
ISBN 0-8070-8337-2 (pbk. : alk. paper)
1. Short stories, Cuban.   2. Cuban fiction—Women authors.
3. Cuban fiction—20th century.   I. Yáñez, Mirta, 1947–   .
II. Cluster, Dick, 1947–   .   III. Schuster, Cindy.
PQ7386.C835   1998
863'.01089287'097291—dc21   97-45924

Contents

contents

question: Define: island.

answer: An island is

an absence of water surrounded

by water: An absence of

love surrounded by

love...

from Dulce María Loynaz, "Geography."

I sit at my desk in Michigan looking out at the autumn leaves on the ground, already brown and withered, and struggle to think of how to begin to define the island from which the stories in this book have come. From my window I see a sky of tarnished silver and feel the impending doom of winter. Back on the island, I imagine, it is balmy. The ocean is warm. A soothing breeze blows. Back on the island, a little girl I know begs to eat an apple, that fruit which is so ordinary in cold northern lands but so rare on the island it can be obtained only with those all-too-scarce dollars. And I, here in the heart of apple country, long for a taste of mango.

(Should I or should I not tell you that my words led to action and I stopped writing to go to the kitchen and devour the overpriced green mango I had been saving like a saint's relic in my refrigerator? This becomes a moment of epiphany. Should I intone the kind of prayer of thanks that I was always being reminded to say as a Cuban immigrant kid growing up in the United States? Okay, I'll say it: For this, yes, my parents left the island, for this my parents came to *La Yuma*, where there's an abundance of everything, *nada falta*, so their daughter could eat a mango out of season without having to share it with anyone).

My editor, Amy Caldwell, who requested I write the foreword, *wants me* to speak personally. So you might say I have permission to speak of apples and mangos. She tells me, "You should draw upon your life as a Cuban-American woman and as a writer to note what you find interesting about the book." Now if that were all, it would be a cinch to write this foreword. But she also wants me to answer questions: "What is the nature of Cuban feminism?" And, "Do the lives of women in Cuba differ from the lives of women in the U.S.?" She tells me that many of the stories suggest that "feminist discourse is fairly new to Cuba," and asks me, "Might you elucidate this state of affairs a bit further?"

I find myself needing to answer such questions the way the great Cuban poet Dulce María Loynaz, who died this year at age ninety-four, answered the question of what is an island. Cuban feminism is a paradox: there are no feminists in Cuba and yet the island is surrounded by feminism.

To understand this paradox we should start with the basics: Cuba is famous for its cigars, its rum, its beaches, and its conga lines, but above all for its women. The myth of the unique eroticism of the Cuban *mulata*, whose heritage is a stunning mix of Spanish and African, goes back to colonial times. But those who speak for the island are always its fast-talking men. In the 1950s no Cuban was more well known than Ricky Ricardo, the clean-cut mambo king of the *I Love Lucy* show, whose indifference to politics and unconcern about his colonized position as a Latino in the United States made him endearing to Americans who viewed

Cuba as their backyard colony. And since the 1960s no Cuban has been as much in the limelight as Fidel Castro, whose warrior manhood and constant need to combat the emasculating power of U.S. imperialism is symbolized by the army fatigues he wears morning, noon, and night; the Americans, after all, imposed a blockade against his island simply because he told them to go to hell, so what's to keep them, one day, from invading?

Before the revolution of 1959 female prostitution was so rampant that just to say the word Cuba was to invoke fantasies of wild and wanton sexuality. Fidel Castro came to power promising to change Cuba's image before the world. And, for a time, he succeeded, turning socialist Cuba into a major player on the world stage during the height of the Cold War. But back on the island, one of his first dramatic gestures was to close the brothels of Havana, which were humiliatingly associated with *yanqui* imperialism and its emasculation of Cuba's men. The "new man" of Cuba would be worthy of Che Guevara's revolutionary idealism, while women would be firm pillars of society, never again forced to work as housewives, maids, and whores. Indeed, Fidel Castro took such a strong interest in "the woman question" that he himself called the feminist revolution in Cuba "a revolution within the Revolution."

Women were organized into a mass organization, the FMC (Federation of Cuban Women), whose founder and president, Vilma Espín, fought in the Sierra Maestra with Fidel Castro and became the wife of his brother Raúl Castro, the head of the armed forces and second in command in Cuba. Espín has repeatedly said that the federation is a "feminine" and not a "feminist" organization: an organization of women committed to a revolution that already speaks in their name. No one can deny that the federation's efforts to combat *machismo* in Cuba have been wide-ranging. With the state providing all women with free education, health care, birth control, access to abortion, nutritional support for pregnant mothers and young children, day care, the freedom to divorce, and the unequivocal defense of women's sexuality in its own right, who needs feminism? The passage of the Family Code in 1975 even legislated many of these rights and formalized the equality of relations between husband and wife in marriage.

The view of Cuban women espoused by the federation was best depicted in a poster from 1979 for International Women's Day which carried the banner, "Woman: Firm, Forever Fighting and Revolutionary" (*La Mujer: Siempre Firme, Combativa y Revolucionaria*). A film made in the same year, *Portrait of Teresa*, sought to put flesh on this ideal by portraying a revolutionary woman who challenges the double standard by leaving her husband because he refuses to agree that men have no more right than women to be unfaithful in marriage. Cuba's high divorce rate, some people say (half in jest, of course), soared after this film! At the same time, the film also suggested that there were obstacles to change when Teresa's mother retorted, "Men will always be men and women will always be women and not even Fidel can change that."

But there is no question that the national desire to transform gender relations, even among those who remained at the margins of the revolutionary project, extended into the personal lives of all women and men. The bold, confident, and fiery voices of the authors represented in this book give more than ample evidence of the strength of Cuban women's search for independence and sexual freedom. And yet feminism in Cuba, as elsewhere in the world, is still an unfinished project. In Cuba, feminism lives and breathes in the shadow of its great male heroes—the independence leader José Martí, the revolutionary martyr Che Guevara, and the Comandante Fidel Castro. Patriarchy has been dismantled without touching a whisker of the beards of the island's patriarchs.

The predecessor to this book, whose original title in Spanish was *Estatuas de Sal (Pillars of Salt)*, invoking the price paid by the biblical Lot's wife, the woman who dares to look, made an impact in Cuba precisely because it offered a collage of Cuban and Cuban-American women's voices that spoke in a feminist language that was refreshingly lacking in didactic fervor or political self-righteousness. The version in English you now hold in your hands is less than half of the contents of the original Spanish, and focuses on the work of a select group of contemporary Cubana writers. But what the volume loses in breadth it gains in intensity, offering a chronicle of the inner desires and disillusionments of Cuban women as well as Cuban men, since many of the authors, interestingly, choose to write from a male point of view. The admirable range of stories, written almost entirely in first person voices, reveal, many of them with the kind of melodramatic flamboyance nurtured by Brazilian and Mexican *telenovelas* so beloved among Cubans, what it means to come from an island called Cuba.

In the last few years there has been a flowering of interest in "*lo cubano*," in all things Cuban—including the Cubanness that takes shape beyond the boundaries of the island. When I went to Cuba in the early 1990s seeking to edit a book about the Cuban cultural arts that would include voices on the island and in the diaspora, such projects were still unusual and looked at with a touch of suspicion both in and outside Cuba. But now my 1995 anthology, *Bridges to Cuba/Puentes a Cuba*, is part of a growing trend, after years of Cold War divisions, toward Cuban efforts at building bridges through art, music, literature, and popular culture. Even this book, decidedly titled *Cubana*, would fall short if it didn't include Cubanas living outside the island. Indeed, there are three stories here by Cuban writers residing in the United States (and the original Spanish included yet another four Cubanas living abroad, among them the recently acclaimed author of erotic fiction, Zoe Valdés, who was on the verge of emigrating to Paris as the Cuban edition went to press).

Cubana appears in the United States just when the brave utopian project of social transformation is unraveling and the last chapter of Cuba's revolutionary history is still being written. With the end of Soviet subsidies that kept the economy afloat and the continuing U.S. trade embargo, Cuba is now entering the global capitalist economy at breakneck speed. Tourism, of the beach and nightclub sort, has returned, and become the Cuban government's main source of hard currency. Add to that the irony that the U.S. dollar, or *el fula*, in popular Cuban speech, is now the only money worth anything and yet Cuban salaries are paid in *pesos*.

Writers, artists, and musicians who gain recognition abroad and travel outside the island are a privileged group. They gain access to dollars and goods not easily available at home, without having to hustle or suffer humiliation. Ordinary Cubans on the island, many of whom had broken off contacts with relatives and friends in Miami once deemed the "worms" and "scum" of the Revolution for leaving the island, have had to swallow their pride and accept the dollars of those in *La Yuma* to be able to buy essentials like soap, cooking oil, and detergent no longer available through the state rationing system. The island's wounded idealism and the lacerating triumphalism of some Miami Cubans make for a tragic counterpoint. Fortunately, at least some Cubans are able to laugh at themselves and convert the pained poignancy of their situation into wry and punning commentary. And so, the Cuban joke goes, the *traidores* (traitors) are now *traedólares* (bringers of dollars).

Cubans, you see, have a history of staying sane by turning everything into a joke, into a *relajo*, and they bring that same lively creativity to their flourishing informal economy, which has arisen alongside the new state capitalist enterprises that include four-star hotels, citrus plantations, Benetton shops, and Volvo, Mercedes, Fiat, and Toyota dealerships funded by foreign investors. People barter whatever they think they might be able to spare, as does the memorable character in Josefina de Diego's monologue, who quips that her dilemma is worse than Hamlet's—"To smoke or to eat, that is the question." But these days the major activity of day-to-day Cuban life is to "invent dollars" by fashioning tourist crafts, running home-based restaurants or *paladares*, and selling just about everything under the sun, from handmade shoes and cigars to perfect replicas of Che Guevara's beret and t-shirts emblazoned with Fidel Castro's image.

The carnivalesque atmosphere is haunted, for feminists, by a bitter reality: Prostitution is back with a vengeance. Foreign men, from Spain, Italy, Germany, Canada, Mexico, and even the United States, go to Cuba again as they did before the Revolution, seeking to play out their wildest pornographic fantasies with beautiful, desperately poor but often highly educated Cuban women. Increasingly, these sexual tourists demand ever-younger Cuban girls, some of whom have not yet celebrated their fifteenth birthday or outgrown their Pioneer uniforms but will trade their tenderness for a Salvation Army dress or a dance at a dollars-only nightclub. Capitalism is arriving in Cuba in many forms, none more savage than that piercing the female body.

National identity is always represented in male terms, which is why Virginia Woolf said that as a woman she had no country, she wanted no country; the world was her country. Indeed, *la patria* is the fatherland. And in Cuba, the male sense of *patria* is heightened by the way manhood and nationhood were fused and confused in the figure of the revolutionary hero.

The current economic and moral crisis in Cuba, together with the sex tourism it has generated, is serving to remind the nation that its women are a most valuable commodity. The crisis has been especially devastating for women because so much was promised them. Despite the vast changes in women's position brought about by the Revolution, it is still the case that most women work a double day, laboring outside the home and carrying the burden of the domestic chores. At a time when the state system can no longer provide the full panoply of services it once so proudly offered, women are turning to their own internal resources, family and neighborhood ties, immense intelligence, and, in some cases, the allure of their own seductiveness to survive.

Wrenching material need, Cuban women are finding, is combined with intense spiritual yearning. In this sense, the current crisis has opened up the possibility for Cubanas to reflect upon the meaning that feminism may now have, to imagine an afterlife without male heroes.

I believe that this book, which is the first collection of short stories by Cuban women to be published in the United States, attempts that reflection, that imagining. Belatedly, perhaps, but *más vale tarde que nunca*, right? It brings together both well-known and new voices, women who range in age from twenty-five to their early sixties, and speaks of things that have never been spoken before in a Cuban context. For if there is any act that is truly heroic for Cubanas at this moment, it is writing. In Cuba housing is terribly scarce. Most of the contributors to this book live with more than one generation of their families and writing is done amidst the ever-present interruptions from relatives and friends as well as the blaring street noise and unforgiving tropical heat. Women writers do not find it easy to retreat to those rooms of their own that Virginia Woolf considered so crucial for women to be able to write. Blackouts and food shortages, and a shrunken publishing world now also heavily dependent on foreign investment, make writing and its circulation difficult, and often impossible. That is the reason why most of the authors represented here cannot dedicate themselves full time to writing; among them are a lawyer, a physiology professor, more than one journalist, a librarian, and a medical doctor. On the other hand, the fact that women of such diverse occupational backgrounds are turning to the pen suggests the importance of creating a space where more voices can be heard.

Obstacles to writing, not only in Cuba but also for Cuban women in the United States, run yet deeper. The question of homeland is so vexed for Cubana writers, and women writers very much need homelands to write, no matter what Virginia Woolf says. For us, truly, the island is an absence of water surrounded by water. Ours is an embattled homeland, divided by revolution and exile; the ocean is our border and bond, the mark of our loneliness and longing.

The U.S. embargo against Cuba limits and oversees contact with the island, allowing only one humanitarian visit a year to Cubans residing here, and requiring that all travel be undertaken with a special license from the Treasury Department that confirms you are not helping to fund the "enemy" with your dollars. It is a challenge for Cubana writers in the United States to maintain the essential contact with the island that they need to express their sense of dual identity. Nor can Cubana writers on the island easily commune, as they increasingly would like to, with their counterparts here. Traveling to Cuba, for Cubans based in the United States, presents its own unique challenges, with the Cuban government putting you through a bureaucratic trial by fire that would have enchanted Kafka. Then there is the blockade imposed by certain sectors of the Cuban exile community, which view any involvement with the island, including family visits, as a collaboration that helps Fidel Castro stay in power. Most painful of all is the internalized blockade, the silencing that takes place on all sides and ends up eating away at those of us who, despite the odds, continue to believe in the importance of open and honest conversations.

But the stories Cubanas are beginning to tell, I believe, can act as a bridge in a divided nation where official channels of communication are blocked by masculine egos and macho politics. It is an interesting coincidence, for example, that the island-based writer Marilyn Bobes and the Chicago-based writer Achy Obejas both confront the taboo, or rather invisible, theme of lesbianism in their stories. Why, I wonder, in both the stories, do the lesbian heroines have to die? Is it because there is no place for them in either of our Cubas?

Male homosexuality in Cuba, in contrast, has a long history of being flagrantly visible. In fact, this so worried the Cuban socialist regime that, in the 1960s and 1970s, special labor camps were created to turn dangerously effeminate men into manly revolutionaries. In his last book, *Before Night Falls* (1990), the writer Reinaldo Arenas writes his memoir as he prepares to commit suicide after developing AIDS in this country. He describes how he fled Cuba in 1980 during the opening of the port of Mariel to escape persecution for being gay and published his work abroad without official permission. Recently, the popular Cuban film *Strawberry and Chocolate* (1993) has offered a more hopeful vision of revolutionary tolerance for gay difference in its depiction of a humane friendship between a young revolutionary named David and a gay critic of the revolution named Diego. While Diego too, like Arenas, must finally leave the island, the film displays unguarded admiration for this gay character's vast knowledge of Cuban literature and art, of which David, the revolutionary, is embarrassingly ignorant. The film even goes so far as to suggest that much of what is great in Cuban culture has been the work of such gay creative artists as José Lezama Lima, Virgilio Piñera, and Ernesto Lecuona, among many others.

There have also been, of course, important gay Cuban women writers and artists, but hardly any—and that includes some of the authors in this book—who would feel safe claiming that identity unambiguously and publicly. Although the gay rights movement has given confidence to lesbian Cubana writers in the United States to be out about their identity, the absence of such a movement in Cuba, and the fact that gayness is so closely associated with men, makes such visibility precarious. Not of course that one must be gay to write about gay characters in literature. The true liberty is when any woman writer can tell the story of a lesbian without having to fix her own identity. So I admire the courage of Marilyn Bobes and Achy Obejas in writing against the grain of this prohibition within Cuban culture, and hope that one day, not too far in the future, other endings, or better yet, other beginnings, will be possible for the lesbian protagonists in their stories. For what is to be desired is not a sentimental vision of lesbian desires or women's intimate friendships, but the full freedom to explore their poignant uncertainty. And that is why I also admire the example set by editor Mirta Yàñez, whose story "Dust to Dust" confronts the secret complicities and terrible betrayals that can accompany women's relationships with each other.

Theirs are not the only risks taken in this book. I also find compelling how the New York–based writer Sonia Rivera-Valdés tries to imagine the frenzy of male desire through a tale so horrendously ribald that it is worthy of Chaucer. Nancy Alonso likewise chooses a male voice for her story in the character of Pepe Cruz, a defeated man who did not have the strength of will to resist the order to throw eggs at a colleague who was leaving the country. I can't help thinking that Alonso's choice of a male character was deliberate, a way of saying how, as a woman, she deplores men's "tooth for a tooth" games, or, to be more exact, their "eggs for eggs" macho politics (*tener huevos*—to have eggs—being Spanish slang for "having balls").

I am intrigued, at the same time, by the efforts of various of the authors to plot women into new life stories. I commend Mylene Fernández Pintado's effort to imagine the kind of intelligent woman protagonist whom men don't like, a woman that has refused to be a mother, a woman that doesn't want clothes "full of drool." In Cuba, where there is no public forum to discuss rape, incest, and sexual abuse, it is admirable that the young writer Ena Lucía Portela is seeking, in an experimental and elliptical way, to depict the inner world of a contemporary female protagonist who can admit to having been beaten by a boyfriend. To be able to plot women into their history is always an essential task for female writers, and so I am drawn to Magaly Sánchez's image of Catalina, a wealthy Cuban woman of the colonial era, who spends long afternoons unabashedly seeking pleasure by voraciously consuming rich foods, intoxicating herself with the scent of jasmine and roses, and pursuing sexual joy with the gardener while her husband Don Diego is away.

And in the present, the as yet barely perceptible present, as consumer goods from *La Yuma* begin inundating the island, I hope more writers will take up the challenge, devilishly assumed by María Elena Llana, of tracing the impact that a package from Miami—consisting of "a hundred and twenty dollars . . . a big Mickey Mouse T-shirt, a pair of tacky bedroom slippers, a few bars of Palmolive, some tubes of Colgate and two sticks of Mum with the magic ball"—can have on the trajectories of those who receive them in Cuba. And as it increasingly becomes possible to speak of some of the phantasmagorical, even absurdist, moments of Cuban socialism, it will be fascinating to hear more stories, like the one told in tongue-in-cheek style by Adelaida Fernández de Juan, in "The Egyptians," about the paranoia that can plague an over-zealous revolutionary consciousness.

These, then, are some of the diverse stories Cubanas are telling—and you can be sure there are many more Cubanas writing stories and many more stories begging to be told.

We are only now just raising the door to that room of our own which is not yet even built.

As I think now of how to end this foreword, I look out at a sunny day, leaves glowing, the sky pale blue, and the thought of winter no longer terrifies me so much.

I remember the seagull that surprised me one morning in an empty parking lot in Michigan. It stood at my feet, also lost, and the ocean, the island, seemed to surround me.

Ruth Behar
October 1997

This foreword was solicited by Beacon Press and does not represent the views of the volume's editor or its contributors.

The footnotes in the introduction, "Voices from the Great Blue River," were originally written in Spanish by Mirta Yáñez. Notes in the stories themselves have been added sparingly by the translators to explain aspects of Cuban life or language that would be obvious to Cuban readers but may be unfamiliar to North American ones.

The translators would like to thank the many people who helped them render these stories into English. Especially: Uva de Aragón, Daniel Barker, Efraín Barradas, Gloria Caballero, Fabiola Carratalá, Tony González, Ena Lucía Portela, Charlie Rosenberg, Susana Sandmann, Mirta Yáñez, and each other.

Introduction

Women's Voices from the Great Blue River

Somewhere in his writings, Ernest Hemingway used the term Great Blue River to describe the Gulf Stream. Hemingway said that he had come to live in Cuba because of the Great Blue River, which offered the best fishing he had ever seen. But for Hemingway, at that time, Cuba was not only fishing. It was an atmosphere that gave density to his stories. It was also the Hotel Ambos Mundos, the Vigía estate in San Francisco de Paula, the Bodeguita del Medio restaurant and its *mojitos*, the Floridita bar and its daiquiris, the friendly isolation in which to write. Cuba was the people and the hubbub necessary to the writer after the dramatic silence of creation, the gravesites of his beloved dogs and cats, the place that offered a pleasant working temperature all year long. And it was the little coastal town of Cojímar, his yacht Pilar, again this Gulf, these shores of the Great Blue River, this sea that forever bewitches those who catch sight of it.

Like almost all writers, Ernest Hemingway was pursuing a truth. For him, the Papa of the Great Blue River, the only proper way of life was to accept challenges. Behind that apparent simplicity hides a worthy philosophy: accept the constant challenge of life and never give up.

The story, the short narrative, has been the most popular representative literary genre in Cuba, especially in the past four decades. What would the great short story writer Ernest Hemingway say about the challenge taken up by Cuban women writers—those living on either shore of the Great Blue River—in writing stories today? Nearly forty years after his death, Cuba continues to be not only a good place to write, but also a fabulous theme. The women writers who live in Cuba or who carry it as part of their baggage have many good stories to tell.

The first Cuban woman who accepted the challenge of narration was the Countess of Merlín (1789–1832). María de las Mercedes Santa Cruz y Montalvo, known as the Countess of Merlín, is most famous as the author of *La Havane* (1844), known in Spanish as "Viaje a La Habana" ("Voyage to Havana"). She lies buried in the Parisian cemetery Père Lachaise. Although her bones do not rest in her beloved Havana, she was the inaugurator of Cuban women's prose.

Since those far-off times in which the Countess of Merlín wrote her celebrated travel chronicles, a lot of water has flowed along the Great Blue River, and more than a few of her successors have "taken the bull by the horns" and set to writing *their* tales.

To write a tale . . . For whatever reasons, in Cuban literature as in that of other countries, the significant female narrative figures first appeared as isolated cases,* but their growing and increasingly persistent presence has covered a wide range of subject matter and esthetics.

---

* In Cuba, female prose writers have been less numerous than female poets, and in this they follow the overall tendency. Likewise, the critical tradition has not escaped the general tendency to make use of a token female.

For an "introduction" to contemporary Cuban fiction—in this case, that written by women—I would like to begin with a few suggestions that lie within the sphere customarily called "literary discourse," which usually stuffs into a single envelope everything which has been and is the province of literary researchers, publishers, professors, critics, and all manner of analysts whose object of interest is "literary production" and its "receptor."

A well-aged assertion from Laurence Sterne's *Tristram Shandy* —although it partakes of the subtly jocular tone in which it is written—presents some illuminating truths: "Writing, when properly managed . . . is but a different name for conversation. As no one, who knows what he is about in good company, would venture to talk all, so no author, who understands the just boundaries of decorum and good breeding, would presume to think all. The truest respect which you can pay to the reader's understanding, is to halve this matter amicably, and leave him something to imagine, in his turn, as well as yourself."* This statement lends itself to multiple interpretations. I want to elaborate upon at least two.

First, literature has as its center the human being, and it implies a dialogue between the objective and the subjective, what Sterne succinctly calls "conversation." He alludes (or I think he does) to the double condition of writing fiction, which reproduces a reality at the same time that it is a product of the imagination. Hence the writer's eternal ambivalence between attitudes of affinity and transgression toward the universe which s/he seeks to capture.

The second interpretation which I want to take from this citation is the quality of "halving the matter," this beloved and never-

* Laurence Sterne, *The Life and Opinions of Tristram Shandy, Gent.* (1760), vol. 2, chap. 11.

enough-pondered *elusiveness*, so difficult to pin down, a mysterious stretch that leads from the real world to the imaginary one, from the concrete to the poetic: the passage that must be traveled between history and its image.

History, image, literature, and language all have no sex, but life experience does, and so does the one transmitting it. In Cuban literary discourse, the stories written by contemporary women—and a good part of those written by our ancestors, a term I use to insist on the size of their legacy—have carried on this "conversation" with the reader, in its double substance of reality and imagination, from a woman's perspective, but (as that gentleman Mr. Shandy would have liked) without "talking all." That is to say, these stories all reveal distinct facets of contemporary Cuban reality, and all share a singular exaltation of the pleasure of reading: that age-old emotion of unique and personal contact between the writer and her better half (if not "better," then worthy and essential), the reader.

The female presence in Cuban narrative can be seen in the most important moments of twentieth-century Cuban literature, with three outstanding figures in each of three distinct tendencies. In the re-creation of the myths of the Afro-Cuban tradition, there is the brilliant intellectual Lydia Cabrera (b. 1900, Cuba; d. 1991, U.S.). In the period known as *criollista*, which gave literary life to the world and speech of the peasantry, Dora Alonso (1910–), writer of short fiction and also of children's books. In the fantastic-philosophical realm, the poet, essayist, and narrator Dulce María Loynaz (1902–97), one of the most distinguished Cuban authors of this century, winner of the 1992 Cervantes Prize.*

---

* A major nineteenth-century figure was the romantic poet, playwright, and novelist Gertrudis Gómez de Avellaneda (1814–73, died in Spain). Important writers of the first half of the twentieth century, besides the three

But female presence is not female consciousness. The consciousness of the female being which tries to appropriate the world in its own way, with knowledge and with neither rage nor feelings of guilt or inferiority, and which seeks to tell the reality or the fantasy unfettered and unconditionally, without borderlines between the "exterior world" and the "interior world"—this is a recent conquest in Cuba.*

Before turning to the new literary production of Cuban women in the 1980s and 1990s, I need to present at least a summary discussion of Cuban literary trends since 1959 and their effects on the presence—or absence—of women's voices.

With the social and structural changes that took place in Cuba after the Revolution of 1959, mature writers and also those beginning their very first drafts had to reconcile the demands of a new social project with the conditions necessary for the act of creation. Cuban literature began to reflect a permanent tension between the conflicts engendered by the social process and the necessity to produce a "useful" art. But the affirmation of an esthetic that would function within the new social project and serve as its historical image resulted in the hegemony of realism. (This process of "imagization" took place not only in literature but also in myths, dreams and chimeras, popular metaphors, leg-

[handwritten margin notes: def. / leadership or dominance, es. / that of one / state or / nation / over / others]

noted in the text, are Renée Méndez Capote (1901–89), Ofelia Rodríguez Acosta (1902–75), Loló de la Torriente (1906–83), Aurora Villar Buceta (1907–81), Loló Soldevilla (1911–71), Iris Dávila (1918–), Mary Cruz (1923–), and Hilda Perera (1926–, living in the U.S.). Note that, for simplicity, a writer's country of residence or place of death is cited only when it is not Cuba.

* Also, in the early decades of this century there appeared a few texts with a somewhat "feminist" approach or defense of women's space, but their formal weaknesses and minor importance keep them from being of much use in constructing an "archeology" of female representation.

ends, and even in the rumors that ran through the streets.) In literature, the choice facing Cuban authors polarized into two extremes, which can be categorized as "the fantastic" and "concrete realism."* At times the extreme forms of these two options led to results that were primitive or naive, even antinomic and exclusionist. The new "realists," impelled at times by extra-literary motives,† ended up consigning to a (symbolic) bonfire everything which departed from their own rigid precepts.

In the early sixties, the first postrevolutionary literary generation began to flex its muscles. Some young writers, male and female, emerged from the intersection of the experimental and the fantastic and for a brief time created work that was not accepted by the dominant realistic canons. Within the new, state-run Cuban National Publishing House, some of these writers published their books in the controversial series "The Bridge," while others published in projects which found oblique ways of escaping mainstream criteria, such as the science fiction series "Dragon." The much-castigated pole of the absurd, black humor, existentialism, the insertion of the unreal or nightmarish into the everyday under the influence of the Argentine writers Jorge Luis Borges and Julio Cortázar—all these forms found their voice among female fiction writers.

---

magical, hard to understand obscure

* Though it took a new form, the division of fiction into an experimental, hermetic tendency and another tendency which embodied varying degrees of realism was not a novelty. This division continued a previous trajectory and paralleled what was occurring on the rest of the continent.

† Parallel to this official posture came actions outside the sphere of writing itself, such as opportunism with the goal of winning jobs or benefits, intolerance toward homosexual writers, centralizing control of literary activities in the hands of a smaller number of individuals, classification of certain subjects as taboo, editorial delays and inefficiency, some writers' emigration, and, among other events that would take too much space to recount in this introduction, polemics and their consequences.

However, there soon came a turning point which most scholars place in 1966, a year that saw the publication of several books that sounded the keynote of the coming times. The title of one of these books gave rise to the name of a current within the field of fiction: *the tough years.** Writers within this current paid exhaustive attention to themes such as the violence that occurs in the crisis of the replacement of one social order by another, specific military confrontations during the Cuban Revolution, and productive work tasks like the cutting of sugar cane.

Women writers aspired to work the difficult soil of the narrative, but because of both sexist "invisibility" and the sudden and extreme tilt of the thematic scales toward "toughness" and violence, they disappeared, with few exceptions, from the literary panorama.†

Thus within the thorny contextual map and the sharp social debate among intellectuals about such topics as the responsibility of the author, it was in narrative fiction—and especially in the story—that the contradictions of this new society first and most clearly took flesh-and-blood form, and this change occurred without the prejudices or morality of the previous era having disappeared. Some of these antagonisms had repercussions on literary works, not only in the sense of creating lasting and valuable texts but also, unfortunately, in the form of obligatory silences and editorial excommunications. Traditionally margin-

---

* *Los Años Duros,* title of a volume of stories published in 1966 by Jesús Díaz, first director of the literary supplement *El Caimán Barbudo,* currently living in Madrid.

† It is enough to take a look at the anthologies of those years—and even more recent ones—at the lists of juries for fiction prizes, and the editorial boards of magazines and other literary institutions, at the catalogues of the various publishing houses, at books of criticism and of essays, and at the records of congresses, book festivals, and other such floral displays.

alized groups, such as gays and women, naturally carried the heaviest burden, to put it euphemistically.

The official standards for the short story—and for other genres—called for the mechanical reproduction of historical events (for example, the description of heroic deeds or one-dimensionally positive characters) and the exaggeration of epic attributes through romantic idealization. "Realism" balanced between the action story and the critical examination of the now-changed past. This "realism," to be achieved at all costs, constituted the stamp of authenticity for the "time of change" through which the nation was passing.* Hence the "sociologizing" emphasis of a great many texts.

The most characteristic stylistic stamps of the era's published works were an insistence on the simplification of language (to the point where works often appear to be bad translations) and of narrative structure; the adoption of cultural syncretism as the identifying trait of Cubanism (for example, the tendency to embrace African or indigenous myths); the recovery of oral traditions and rural themes; a tendency to stay away from essences, to evade conflicts and create cardboard characters; the poorly elaborated influence of Russo-Soviet narrative, of Dreiser, Dos Passos, and Hemingway, and some Latin American fiction writers (especially the Mexican Juan Rulfo); stereotypical dialogue in which popular speech was transferred mechanically to the page (for instance, the repeated rendition of *para allá* as *p'alla*);† and trans-

---

* "Time of change" was another term coined at this time, in this case to describe the transition to a better, utopian world through a confrontation of values that would result in the critical demolition of the previous historical era. Targets of this criticism were such elements as prostitution, gambling, machismo, racism, and religious belief. The late Manuel Cofiño used the expression as the title of one of his works (*Tiempo de Cambio*, 1969).

† Gabriel García Márquez has noted that in dialogue, what works in English (for instance, for Hemingway) does not work in Spanish, that Spanish speech must be elaborated in a different form to feel true.

parent plots presented without philosophical questions. The female writers did not escape, of course, from these stylistic infelicities.

In this climate, themes of love and fantasy were avoided. Complexities were shunned in the sphere of ideas and in the formal sphere as well. For young women writers the situation was especially difficult. They were too young to write about the vices of the past. They lacked models, since many of their recent predecessors did not fit the literary requirements of the new times. And, although they had shared the same vicissitudes as the young men of their generation, the epic primacy accorded to the underground struggle, military training and combat, and barracks life left the majority of women writers on the margins of the literary frontier.

Thus the discourse of "toughness," and in general a large part of the subject matter under discussion, placed women's narrative in a disadvantaged situation not only with respect to experience and plot elements, but to the hegemonic body of narrative whose publication was prioritized by official taste. Yet, against time and tide, women writers sporadically made their presence felt in the short story genre, with books, prizes, and publication in magazines.

In the early seventies, the conflict between literary tendencies grew sharper. The anthologies of fantasy stories disappeared, names were erased from literary dictionaries and academic courses, and literary workshops inculcated in their students the "best way to write about real reality." Many of the champions of these witchhunts (and of course wizard-hunts) have disappeared from view. What is most amazing is that the search for a popular and "realistic" literature gave rise to the paradox of a "realism" that was unconvincing.

During these so-called "five years of gray" (in my view, almost

ten) many mediocre books appeared, their authors having en-
listed in a tropical "socialist realism" which did not manage to
gain as many adherents as some would have liked. Some of its the-
orists and practitioners hid their formal weaknesses behind the
pursuit of a literature for a so-called majority or behind a false di-
dacticism. They clung to that rhetoric which had shown itself to
lead to success or easy acceptance. Readers, who are never wrong,
have forgotten them. (Naturally, even during this period, some
brilliant exceptions were published.)

The end of the seventies saw a continuing emphasis on things
of the surface. There was a gradual shift from a speechifying
mode to more reflective interpretation, but many writers kept
within the constraints of a flattening realism that was more given
to exterior anecdote than to the examination of the interior being.
Some writers justified this orientation in terms of the difficulties
of capturing such a turbulent reality. The zeal for formal experi-
mentation (which, although at times it failed to jell, had at least
bubbled through the fiction of the sixties) had almost completely
disappeared.

During this time, Cuban literature written in exile began to make
itself known—the opposite side of the coin from the literature of
"change." This was the other shore of the Great Blue River of Cuban short fiction: stories written outside of Cuba by authors who
emigrated or who were born in other countries, such as the United
States, Puerto Rico, and Spain. The most dazzling female figure
among these writers was Lydia Cabrera. Other authors left Cuba
as young women and did not continue publishing; their earlier
texts published in Cuba belong to the legacy which gave rise to
current Cuban female discourse. New names have emerged, as

have books written in an intermediate language, or completely in English, the language of the country where some have been raised. The examination of this complex phenomenon has begun only very recently, on both sides of the Great Blue River.

From my point of view, the search for an identity, or the natural incorporation into the creative process of the particularizing elements of our Cuban idiosyncrasy, is one of the unifying traits of Cuban narrative. This search reveals a continuity with previous narrative writing, and it marks the character of Cuban narrative on *both* shores. The writers who left and continue living abroad belong, whether they like it or not, to the current of Cuban literature of this century. This is the rich situation of our literature, torn apart in its diversity yet constant in its unity.

We also find on both shores the theme of Cuba as a meeting of cultures, a mixture not only of African and Hispanic ingredients but also of the closest and most influential Western culture, the North American, together with the recognition and defense of the Cuban identity as a part of Latin America. This theme has introduced new elements into the eternal dilemma of Cubanism versus universality, at times resolved neither by the authors nor by the critics. But is this a dilemma, I ask? I think that, without falling into the homogenizing blandness of postmodernity or the stereotypical rigidity of *tojosismo*,* we can now accept that all the ingredients of the multifarious stew which in Cuba we call *ajiaco* have formed a distinctive mass. The tip of this tropical iceberg may be the famous names (Alejo Carpentier, José Lezama Lima, Dulce María Loynaz, and Virgilio Piñera among others), but be-

---

* *La tojosa* is a bird characteristic of the Cuban countryside, whose repeated appearance in trite verse and rural narrative gave rise to the satirical term *tojosismo* to refer to a forced Cubanism bulging with references to the tojosa, the palm tree, maracas, and the like.

low that tip an abundant and skilled body of Cuban authors has been solidifying. These authors come from all generations, sexes, colors, and localities, and they form an original, varied, and intense literary group within the historical Latin American community that José Martí called one America unique and indivisible.

In the first half of the eighties, in Cuba, something new began to appear in literature. Because these new stories revealed events from a subjective point of view which was usually that of a child or adolescent character, and also because they made use of the resources of so-called magic realism, critics refer to the production of this period as "dazzled stories."*

A number of female writers published their first books at this time, in some cases breaking ground for this style of "astonishment." If they still lacked clear consciousness of a gendered point of view,† these women began to join collective problems with the particulars of their gender and (along with some of the best of their male colleagues) to dismantle the conflicting extremes, without allowing themselves to be frightened by traditional writers who continued to work in the old epic and heroic style.

The fundamental obligation to leave marginality behind, and the urgency of breaking with dogmas foreign to literature, caused women writers to be the first to go beyond the Manichean vision

---

* *Cuentística de deslumbramiento.* It is not yet possible to undertake a thorough critical review of the nomenclature that has been applied to all the post-1959 developments: *realistas, esteticisistas, violentos, exquisitos, deslumbrados, tojosistas, novísimos, del cambio, de la cotidianeidad, de adentro, de afuera, los duros, los blandos* . . . It will take some time for this cacaphony to settle into tune.

† Within the debates about women in Cuba, only very recently has criticism begun to adopt a gender perspective. The terms "feminine," "feminist," and others of this type are still proscribed in literary criticism.

and devote themselves to developing a more complex form of representation. These short story writers began to present a discourse (sometimes poetic, sometimes crude) of the reconfiguration of values and customs previously seen as immutable. They unveiled the interior world and demystified personal life, without lowering their voices when it came time to speak about the female body (or the male one) and sexual relations. They challenged the horsemen of the apocalypse patrolling the border between genres, including the worst of these, which is self-censorship. They took on "conflictual"* themes such as marginality or generational conflict that include criticism of the society and of sacred and accepted institutions—among them, marriage.

In the nineties a definitive opening toward new or previously excluded themes began. The key thing: the new writers—and some others who rediscovered their paths after straying from them—neither had to purposefully strive for popular language nor to prove at all costs that they were "cosmopolitan."

With the entry of parody and intertextuality, deeper interest in human relationships, and the recovery of urban settings in rejection of the "sociologizing" required in previous periods, Cuban short fiction in general—and especially that written by women—was moving away from the epic and from narrow realism.

The astonishment of the "dazzled stories" is gone, I would say. Rather, the story assumes an interest in the internal world of its characters, in their troubles, and in the internal relations of the family as well. The protagonists become more human, interest in the city reappears, writers take up "conflictual" themes such as marginalized youth, homosexuality, emigration, and the diffi-

---

* The word *conflictivo* belongs to Cuban language. It alludes not only to what is controversial or polemical, but also to what departs from the standard, what might lead to problems, what breaks with the conventional.

culties of Cuban life today. There are good doses of existential-ism, black humor, the absurd, and the erotic, among quite a few other violations of the previous standards.

As the esthetic of "the tough years" is left behind, the walls be-tween the fiction written by women and "the other fiction" (that accepted by the dominant discourse) are being torn down. This is not to say that such participation in the esthetic current of their epoch impedes a specifically female literary representation or a consciousness of female ways of being.

The selections in this anthology include authors from both shores of the Great Blue River.* Hemingway would have enjoyed seeing how Cuban women writers have accepted all the challenges of telling their own stories. Their fiction reveals an intuitive blend-ing of Sterne's long-ago advice to avoid telling all (a requirement of an entertaining conversation) and a very particular incorpora-tion of the Hemingwayesque code whose essence is glorification of the often solitary struggle for existence, and therefore for death. In many of Hemingway's works, a man fights alone (and

---

* For a larger panorama, see Mirta Yañez and Marilyn Bobes, eds., *Esta-tuas de sal: cuentistas cubanas contemporáneas* (Havana: Ediciones UNION, 1996). That volume includes, in addition to stories by writers rep-resented or mentioned here, stories by Marta Rojas, Lourdes Casal, Omega Agüero, Evora Tamayo, Josefina Toledo, Olga Fernández, Ana María Simo, Nora Macía, Excilia Saldaña, Enid Vian, Ruth Behar, Gina Picart, Chely Lima, and Verónica Pérez Kónina.

Some studies of Latin American women's writing make mention of Cu-ban writers who have won renown outside of Cuba after long stays in other countries, such as Julieta Campos and Aralia López González in Mexico, Nivaria Tejera in France, Cristina García in the U.S., and, most recently, Zoe Valdés. I also regret omissions that have occurred out of ignorance, copy-right problems, and limitations in accessibility or space. I would very much have liked to include Mayra Montero.

almost always dies alone). In response to the question of why, the narrator simply answers that no one can fully know. This is the source of that tone so many have tried but failed to imitate: that special manner of confronting human tragedy with a strange mixture of coarseness, tenderness, and humor.

These Cuban women writers—with humor, tenderness, and sometimes coarseness as well—send their protagonists (almost always female) to face the struggle for existence. Not hunting a tiger or advancing against the enemy under a rain of bombs, but fighting life's daily battles. And the code is the same: accept the challenge and never give up.

Literary criticism has classified Ernest Hemingway as a twentieth-century romantic hero, but this categorization, applying the labels of bygone eras, does not completely explain how Hemingway could become the emblem of a much more contemporary attitude. Might it be the enormous need for adventure that we all carry inside us? Might it be that one of the most-quoted phrases in literature—"a man can be destroyed but not defeated"—is an irreplaceable motto for meeting life's challenge with dignity? It will do for women as well. These writers confirm that.

Here is the voice of Cuban female discourse in sixteen authors. Some began to write in the sixties, others in the difficult seventies. But almost all the stories presented here were written between the second half of the eighties and today.

In all these writers we find a consciousness of gender. The female voice now appears consciously, regardless of whether the point of view is situated in female or male characters. The undertow from the passions of the sixties—and the gray of the seventies—are replaced by reflection, anti-epic, and a determination to present a vision of reality which is neither Manichean nor "realist." There is no longer a propagandistic stance in descriptions of society, but instead a pure verification of the invisible forces that drive our lives. The major common element in these sixteen stories is irony. And something else, a tone that we could call "tough," from the open violence of death to the hidden violence of coexistence and the vicissitudes of daily life. As one of the anthologized writers might put it: the circumstances of that "place for fallen angels."* Are we in the presence of more "tough years," this time seen from a female point of view? But, while there are areas of common interest among these sixteen writers, their styles are most diverse.

Marilyn Bobes, in "Somebody Has to Cry," takes on one of the great taboos of the past decades (sexual prejudices in an imperfect society), while her use of minor key, fragmentation, and changing points of view provide a good sampling of her narrative skills. María Elena Llana assures me that her story "Japanese Daisies" was written some years ago, but the crude language and the tackling of a sordid reality could convince us that it is much more recent (why not think that writers have premonitions like anybody else?). Josefina de Diego abandons the delicate tone of her first book (of reminiscences) to present a soliloquy that gives a fierce-yet-tender image of difficult daily life; its title, "Internal Monologue on a Corner in Havana," displays the irony and the painful humor that are very much the author's own. In "A Tooth for a Tooth," Nancy Alonso offers the apathetic a strong slap in the face; her tale accepts the challenge of traditional story structure in the interest of bearing reflective, sharp, and sensitive witness to the drama of contemporary Cuban life.

Mylene Fernández Pintado has a sharp eye for detail and works from the marrow of her female identity; in "Anhedonia (A Story

---

* See María Elena Llana, "Japanese Daisies."

in Two Women)," she unveils the intimate universe of two women whose destinies seem to both confront and complement each other. Aida Bahr also keeps a focus on the world of women in "The Scent of Limes," a story of turbulent passions told by a young girl in a context of racial, moral, and religious conflicts; under its quiet surface, a strong charge of violence steadily builds. Neatly and with an economy of means, Esther Díaz Llanillo gives us in "My Aunt" an ambiguous vision of old age and the presence of the dead among the living, while Ana Luz García Calzada, in "Disremembering a Smell," offers a new form of *criollista* literature: the story's charm lies in its combination of the "naturalistic" and the symbolic. Setting her story "Catalina in the Afternoons" in colonial times, Magaly Sánchez makes use of a linguistic precocity that ironically recreates the past; she narrates the classic discovery of pleasure with an unexpected twist: the act of love consummated with a bird. Rosa Ileana Boudet's "Potosí 11: Address Unknown" is a completely confessional text, a naked reflecting interior self, which, simultaneously, portrays an external space that is rich in references yet equally disembodied; whether it is a monologue, a dialogue with no visible response, or yet again something else, its perception of human behavior is profound. Sonia Rivera-Valdés depicts an eroticism both disconcerting and grotesque; her monologue "A Whiff of Wild Desire," addressed to a particular listener, also functions to establish a link between identity and *el cubaneo.**

Mirta Yáñez, it has been said, insists on viewing life without inhibitions or much in the way of logic, but her care to design a par-

---

* *Cubaneo* is a term used in various contexts in which its connotation ranges from applause to condemnation. It alludes to a certain body of Cuban characteristics and idiosyncracies, specifically, as I see it, referring to collective behaviors. Some authors limit its frame of reference to festive behavior, but I think the range is broader than that.

ticular atmosphere, her attention to language, some ethical anxi-
eties, and a tone of (black?) humor would be the best clues for
readers of her story "Dust to Dust" to pursue. Uva de Aragón,
whose characters are in desperate straits, shows the humanist side
of our complex contemporary life, a life that justifies polemic,
rage, and fear; "I Just Can't Take It" is one of the most wrenching
stories in this book. Adelaida Fernández de Juan, on the other
hand, supplies a note of subtle humor in her graceful story "The
Egyptians." Ideal for paranoiacs, it's a satirical (and devastating)
look at the ups and downs of Cubans working abroad. The out-
spoken émigré narrator of Achy Obejas' "We Came All the Way
from Cuba So You Could Dress Like This?" examines the differences between her own and her parents' attitudes, whether toward Cuba or toward conventional sexual morality. And Ena
Lucía Portela's "The Urn and the Name (A Lighthearted Tale)"
dives into a murky world whose characters adopt an inclusive morality of their own. It is a story that does justice to its author's experimental aims, as the atomized narration develops from a simple anecdote and gathers density through the references in which
it is enveloped.

These writers, these voices from both shores of the Great Blue
River, have Cuba as their common core and their grand plot. Even
when it does not make itself explicit in the narrative content, it is
there in the perspective, the point of view, the distance that intervenes when they are describing other cultures, the tone, the joy
and the pain of the things portrayed, the language, and—even for
those who write in another tongue—in the Cuban rhythm and
cadence of their words.

The writers defend Cuban identity, and they defend the female
perspective (the woman's voice), projecting these qualities and
putting them forward as common and as their own. To my mind,

the most outstanding characteristic of the Cuban women writers of today (present in the sixteen authors of this anthology) is our *special* realism: a realism that the Cuban story writers have shaped by broadening the spectrum of the everyday, adding the absurd, the magical, the supernatural, humor, fantasy, and nonsense to daily life, with the political scene, society, and ideas as a backdrop. In the foreground are human beings with their struggles and their "strugglets."* Almost all of these writers achieve a synthesis between the register of intimate memories and that of historical testimony, between objectivity and subjectivity, adding a certain melodramatic touch *a lo cubano* as well.

The writers of this Great Blue River (and I too like to call it that because it isn't so much a maritime current that separates us, as a river in full flood that unites) are also connected in ethical purpose, in the personalization of conflict, and in the consciousness of that social space, always present one way or another, which is Cuba.

That Great Blue River also joins us in alliance with the reader, that Great Blue River, the same Gulf current whose force and whose beauty draw us all along.

Mirta Yáñez
May 1997
Havana
Translated by Dick Cluster

---

* *Luchitas*, a term that is almost untranslatable because it refers to almost everything that makes up the behavior, thought, and experiences of Cubans.

Marilyn Bobes was born in 1955. A professional journalist, she won the David Prize for poetry in 1979 in Cuba,
and prizes for narrative in Mexico and Peru in 1994. Her
book of stories *Somebody Has to Cry* won the Casa de las
Américas prize in 1995. She is also the author of two books
of poetry, *Someone Is Writing with Tenderness* (1978) and
The Needle in the Haystack (1979), and co-editor of the anthology of Cuban women's stories *Pillars of Salt* (1996).
"Somebody Has to Cry" is from the collection of the same
name.

Translated by Dick Cluster

Somebody Has to Cry

daniel

She's almost in the middle, smiling. Really she's the most beautiful, though she didn't know it then. She didn't even dare imagine
it. Her nose bothers her; maybe it's too big for a girl of fifteen.
With time, her face will arrange itself and nothing will be out of
proportion, nothing to mar it. But right now the present is all she
cares about.

On her right, Alina, who has already got a pair of enormous
breasts. She's the *criollita*, the curvaceous prize that all the junior
high boys desire and incessantly pursue. Cary envies her a little,
not knowing that twenty-four years later all that will remain of

the imposing Alina is a woman who is fat, flabby, and sad. Alina doesn't know it either and maybe that's why, in the year 1969 that's frozen in the photo, she's standing on tiptoe above the others, proud of all her volume, her splendor, usurping the space of the rest, relegating them to second best.

On the far left, fuzzy from the back lighting, Lázara is hard to make out: thin thighs, graceless figure, mousy face. Her chest is still flat and innocuous. She raises her eyes to the camera as if begging pardon for her existence. That's Lázara a few months before the tragedy. Afterward she dropped out of school. She couldn't stand the looks, the laughter, the reputation that came along with an unsanctified pregnancy in junior high in those years. The flight of The Old Man topped it off—he was the guy in his forties who used to wait for her outside the school in the little park, and with whom she would trustingly disappear into The Woods. Next to Cary, also to the left, two unidentified girls. They look alike; you'd almost call them twins. Short, round, with dolls' eyes, they're present only so that behind them, above their bangs and their heads and their small happy destinies, Maritza can appear. Her powerful frame, rising over the group, is an aggressive presence in the portrait.

Time, working on the photo, has turned Maritza's eyes transparent. She already seems marked for death. She doesn't look at the camera. She doesn't smile. She's the only one not putting on a birthday face. Her broad shoulders reveal the athlete, the champion in free-style for four straight seasons. She's also beautiful, although in a different way. Her face was perfect and mysterious, like no other in the photo, like there may never be in Havana again.

cary

They found her drowned. Like a character in an ephemeral soap opera: an overturned glass and a half-empty bottle of rum on the bathroom floor, an inch or two away from the hand that hung over the edge of the tub. The remains of the pills in the mortar, still there on top of the sink, and the wrinkled wrappers in the trash.

At the wake, a man whose face seemed familiar said that it didn't seem like a woman's suicide. Except for the pills. It seemed too rational: predicting the deep sleep from the barbiturates, the downward slide until her back rested on the bottom and water irreversibly filled her lungs. I suspect what bothered him was the idea of Maritza's nude body exposed to the eyes of a dozen curious onlookers waiting for the Forensic Medicine technicians to arrive.

But Maritza never had any sense of modesty like that. She would be the first to arrive at the sports complex and, before opening her locker, she'd yank off her blouse, step out of her skirt, and start doing knee bends and sit-ups in an explosion of uncontrollable energy. Her legs and torso, their muscles strong and well-knit, whirled compulsively before our eyes. I remember that once she'd finished her exercises, she'd put a stretch cap over her short hair and, completely nude, disappear into the showers with the stride that was so much her own: long, confident, slow.

Unlike us, she didn't care much about her image. Now that time has gone by and I see things differently, it occurs to me that she cultivated her body for its use-value.* All the rest of us, even if

---

* Marxist economics makes a distinction between use-value (what a good or service is worth in terms of utility) and exchange-value (the price at which it can be bought or sold).

we devoted ourselves to gymnastics or swimming, were preparing ourselves for a future auction; one way or another, we were always on display.

Lázara, Alina, and I tortured ourselves daily with cinched-up belts and tight pants. Maritza was happier; she disguised herself with loose outfits, slightly strange ones, as if stubbornly trying to come in last. We scolded her more than once for her laxness and, sometimes, for her lack of modesty too: when she sat down she'd never pull at the hem of her miniskirt or strategically locate her pocketbook on her thighs as the rest of us did. I don't even remember her carrying a pocketbook. She'd leave the house with a beat-up wallet, made by some anonymous artisan, that would barely hold her identity card and some cash. Lots of times, as we walked, she'd ask Alina to keep it in her shoulder bag full of perfume, tissues, lipsticks, eyeliners, and all the other makeup imaginable.

alina

She always had it inside her. Always. More than once it occurred to me and I was on the point of warning Cary. That nerviness about going around naked, those indecent theories, that mania about controlling her . . . I don't know why we didn't discover it in time. We were normal, we dressed well, we thought the way women think.

That thing with my husband, she didn't do it just to bother me, but for God knows what other dirty reasons. Nonetheless, she paid for it. You pay for those things.

He couldn't manage anything with her. He told me this morning in the funeral parlor. There was something strange in the way she took off her clothes, something brazen. And afterward, she humiliated him. She got dressed again as if it were nothing, she didn't want explanations, she said goodbye with a nasty look and even dared to crack a cynical joke: And now, what are you going to do if I decide to tell Alina about this?

He confessed all that in an attack of sincerity and rage, so I wouldn't be moved, so I wouldn't get sucked in by Lazarita's weakness and put my name on the wreath. No, I won't allow it. Maybe Caridad and Lázara don't care what people say, but we do. We did enough by coming to the wake. We're not going to the funeral. Politeness has its limits.

It's true that I let myself go. The childbirths did me in, they ruined me, it's true. But how could I think about my figure? The woman who doesn't have children never feels fulfilled. Lots of them, like Maritza, like Cary, stay in better shape because they don't give birth. I was brought up differently, to have a family. I'm not sorry. I love my children very much, and nothing could have replaced the joys they've given me. That's what completes a woman: a family.

I decided that they were sacrificing all this because they liked to show off. If they'd had to cook, wash, iron, and take care of a house, they would have had trouble finding the time to read books and daydream. Cary figured that out. She's spent her life divorced. But Maritza . . . Now it's clear why she wasn't interested in marriage or stability. In her case, the answer was much simpler.

I was dumb. If they surprised me at a bad moment, I'd let it all out, telling them things I didn't even think. I was still young and immature. I didn't have to tell them what went on between me and my husband. Maritza didn't have to see me crying. Why should I have given them that pleasure? Over time, I came to understand that it's normal. It happens in all marriages, that passion turns into companionship, into peaceful and lasting affection.

Even if they need a little affair once in a while, a wife is a wife. The woman they chose to marry. The question of sex becomes secondary when one matures.

Nonetheless, it hurt me. Maritza always tried to compete with me, to outdo me in some way. In '72, on a voluntary work brigade, she managed to be a finalist in the Tobacco Queen contest. Of course, it was me who won. The head of the rural Plan, three farmers, and the high school principal were the judges. The principal and one of the farmers voted for her. But the rest of the judges and the public were on my side from the beginning. She could never be my equal. In spite of her pretty face and that reputation she cultivated by playing hard to get. She knew it was the mystery that made her interesting, and she managed to keep it going for a long time. In our junior year at the University she was still a virgin. Or at least, that's what people said.

I had to put up with her day after day at the University too. When she knew I wanted to study architecture, that's where she went and enrolled. So I know her better than anyone. I put up with a lot from her. Especially her envy. The only thing I wouldn't accept was her attempt to dominate me. She didn't like that, and the friendship ended then and there. We had a falling out.

I feel like I can still see her, acting humble but really being so arrogant underneath. That little voice, syrupy and halfway hoarse, and her affected vocabulary. She wore herself out with interviews, letters, and meetings, thinking that someone was going to take an interest in her thesis: alternative building styles. She was a snob. So many people needed houses and she worried about diversity, about reconciling functionality, available resources, and esthetics. She ruined a whole New Year's Eve with that litany. I don't know why we invited her. It was Lazarita's idea, or Cary's.

Everybody trying to enjoy themselves, and her sitting in the

easy chair like an English lady, monopolizing their attention. And
Cary kept giving her more and more rope, so she'd keep talking.
Even Lázara was taken in by her nonsense. Something Maritza
said seemed to her like the height of genius: that getting up every
morning and looking at identical buildings makes people intoler-
ant, predisposes them against differences. Poor stupid Lázara was
impressed by that foolishness. She always had a complex about
the supposed intelligence of Maritza and Cary. The two of them,
especially Maritza, filled her head with pretensions when she was
still a girl. And now what? She can't keep a man. Not just because
she's ugly, but because she's dumb. I've seen many uglier than her
who are married now. It's because she doesn't learn. She chases
them, and then right away she opens her legs. She confesses that
she wants to marry them. Nothing scares a man more than the
feeling that you want to trap him. That's why The Old Man left
her high and dry. He left her burdened with a fatherless daughter,
to this day. I got really tired of repeating myself. What you've got
to do with men is show them indifference, drive them to distraction and make them think they're the ones making the decisions.
I'm not going to waste more breath on her. Let her keep being led
by Cary, she'll see. Cary has been married three times and has had
as many boyfriends as she's wanted, but poor Lázara . . . nothing
happens for her. And at forty, not even Marilyn Monroe can get a
guy to marry her.

daniel

I met Lázara at work. I knew from the way she looked at me that
she'd put out easily and that later it would be easy to get rid of her
as well. She had too low an opinion of herself to become one of
those stubborn, clinging women who refuse to accept the fact that

when they cross paths with a man by chance, their condition is going to be volatile, ephemeral, and without roots. In her sad flirtation devoid of charm or pride, there was a resignation to the fleeting nature of any bond she might make. I liked that about her. That and the harebrained idea that she might be good in bed.

Sometimes not-very-attractive women can be really surprising when you get intimate with them. As if they want to make up for what they lack with daring and imagination. Besides, I was alone and bored, and New Year's was coming up.

That New Year's Eve, Lazarita was invited to a party. When I agreed to go too, her face lit up with a joy that seemed excessive. It was clear that she'd spent too many New Years' alone, and to show up with me (at that house where "her lifelong friends" would be), was a coup, a boost for her self-esteem.

We'd already gone out two or three times before. I'd found her drab, trembling body to be pleasant, but I could see it wouldn't amount to more than that. In the middle of January I was scheduled for a trip to the provinces and I was planning to leave Lázara for good then, without hurting her too much, taking advantage of the forced separation plus other pretexts, postponements, and pious white lies.

But that New Year's Eve I met what Lázara called "her lifelong friends." Among them was Alina, whose house it was: a fat housewife with three children and of no interest to me. But there was also Maritza, who was an impressive woman: something like a Pallas Athena in the middle of that silly room crammed with macramé. She gave the impression of being untouched and, nonetheless, seemed experienced too. And, above all, there was Cary. Cary, on the far end of the sofa, attentively following Maritza's explanations—about architecture, I think. She was holding a glass of rum in one of her thin, aristocratic hands, while she indolently surrendered the other to a man I instantly disliked. Cary: her fine, angular face, her eyelids always blinking because of her lenses, her delicate mouth, her body, her skin. All meticulously crafted by a goldsmith: for love, to be kissed, touched, and sipped inch by inch.

cary

We went to movies, cafeterias, and parties, but Maritza preferred the beach. Any time of year, even winter. I was the only one who would go with her on those cold, gray days. We enjoyed a very pleasant privacy that you could never find in August.

On the deserted reefs we'd undo our bikini tops and each anoint the other's back with the mixture of cooking oil and iodine which we used to cope with the lack of store-bought tanning cream. Along a stretch of the coast which we called La Playita, Maritza and I talked a lot. With a sincerity I never felt with the others, I told her all about the setbacks in Alejandro's and my engagement, which I shed so many useless tears for. She listened with a careful attention that I've never found in anybody else since.

Maritza understood me. Nonetheless, it irritated her that I should waste so much time and energy analyzing in such detail—obsessively, she said—something so insubstantial. She had a hard time accepting that I could convert my relationship with Alejandro into something central and decisive, that this pastime was so absorbing as to erase the interest and satisfaction of all others—writing, for example. She was sure I'd become a writer, especially after I told her about my diaries. Since I was girl, every night before going to sleep, I've written my impressions of the day in a notebook. I'm still surprised that one of those afternoons I let

Maritza read a few pages—the ones I thought were the best written and most intense.

Maybe, without knowing it, I had been looking for a reader. Maritza seemed so interested, she encouraged me so much, that I couldn't resist the temptation to show her those entries in spite of the fact that, until then, I'd considered my diary sacred and inviolable. I kept it hidden under my pillow.

I remember that she praised my gift for description and the supposed keenness with which I presented details. The only thing she didn't like was that (there too) the leading character was Alejandro. Because her criticisms hurt, I defended myself by trying to undercut her argument with my experience: maybe she would understand when she fell in love. And then she told me that she too had once thought she was in love. But love, she told me, is too uncertain and changeable a sentiment. We shouldn't give it the central role that only the most essential things deserve.

At seventeen, Maritza already thought that the more fulfilled a person felt, the less she needed another person in order to be happy. Love, she insisted, is an arrangement between losers. That's why it's almost always we women who are most in love. Because women by nature are the ones who lose.

We've been brought up, she told me once, to clear the way for the triumph of men: look at you, with all your talent, and all you talk about is them.

Maritza always broached those subjects very naturally, without any dramatizing, and avoiding solemnity. Suddenly, as if the conversation no longer interested her, she would jump up and, after refastening her bikini straps, she'd give me a complicitous tap on the shoulder and dive into the sea. From there she'd begin joking about Alejandro and making fun of my sufferings with so much wit that, many times, they'd seem ridiculous and false even to me.

alina

Maritza could talk you into anything. She had this tricky, lawyer-ish quality that Cary never did. Nobody high up listened to her, but other people, even intelligent ones like my own husband, looked at her as if they were seeing an extraterrestrial. It's true that, on that night, she came very well dressed. When she began working, she started to enjoy dressing up. She made herself up like a queen and she had that bronzed skin that you only see in magazines. She always managed to seem prettier than she really was.

I'm sure that on that New Year's Eve she came with the intention of taking my husband away. And then I had to hear her complain that men never listened to her: they invited her to lunch, supposedly because they were interested in her project, and ended up inviting her to sleep with them. That's not the way I see it. She provoked them herself. Maybe if she'd said yes to just one of them, Havana would be full of alternative buildings. I mean, if she was able to do it to my husband, why not one of those functionaries too?

That's what she was into in '83 or '84. I think those were her best years. Because we have to be honest: she didn't seem like what she was. You would have had to be very suspicious to notice those few details. For instance, I never liked her manner of dragging out her s's—the way they do.

The indications are that sometime after we stopped seeing each other, she started to drink a lot. Not in public, but in private. At the wake, her neighbor said that Maritza would go into the apartment every day with a bottle of wine or Havana Club in her shopping bag.

In the afternoons, after her bath, she'd sit on the terrace in a pair of shorts and a little white top to listen to Brazilian music and drink. Alone. Completely alone.

They never saw her with any men. When the other woman moved in with her, everybody thought it was a relative or a very close friend. The woman had a child. That boy must have been the reason she decided to go back to her husband. Poor thing. I can't imagine how people can sacrifice their children to go indulge their deviant behavior.

Maritza fell into a deep depressive state. She stopped greeting the neighbors and she quit her job.

I didn't see her again until today: old and blue, through the glass of the coffin. It was a very unpleasant spectacle. Caridad seemed like a zombie, completely transformed. I had never seen her like that, not even over men, which is the problem that destabilizes her most. When they took the body away she blanched and if my husband hadn't held her tight I think she would have fainted right there. Right in front of everyone, giving people grounds to think badly of her. And by association, of us. I had to speak to her harshly to get her to react. Finally, I said: a woman like Maritza, with no children, no man, and her pathology, what does she have to live for? It's like if you give birth to an abnormal child—even though it's yours, it's better if it dies, right? She made a decision and she had reasons to commit suicide. Cary, don't you see that?

lázara

Now that they've taken her away, and now that Alina has left with all the hate she's got inside her that turns a person evil like Odette or like Fatima or like Justina, the maid in the other soap opera, now I'm going to cry as much as I want. Because I don't believe that Maritza liked women that way. And if she did, it was her business. She didn't hurt anybody, being like that. But no. I know perfectly well that she wasn't attracted to women. It's just that she was so good. She shared everything. She didn't keep anything for herself. I remember that when her father brought her those orange patent leather shoes from Hungary, she gave them to me. I didn't have any good shoes. But I didn't want her to deprive herself. I was ashamed. Then Maritza told me: you're going to enjoy them more than me. And I think that was true. She didn't care about things, but about people's happiness. She got so happy when my girl would say, Aunt Maritza, take me to the aquarium. She would take her, she'd explain the habits of the fish, she'd tell her that story about the lonesome seal that she made up. I even liked it myself. It hurts Cary a lot too, that she should kill herself. Just like that, overnight, as if she were a bad person who didn't deserve to live. Everybody knows Maritza didn't make trouble for anyone. And if she wanted to build those houses, that wasn't for herself but for other people. For me too. Wouldn't you like to live in one of these, she asked me once, showing me a drawing she had made for her job. She didn't need those houses. She lived very well. In a very pretty apartment, elegant, full of plants and paintings and with decorations outside. I never saw her look at us with any improper intentions or anything like that. On the contrary.

Even Daniel, that strange man who went out with me for about two months, liked her a lot. He behaved very well. He stayed at the funeral parlor all day. He was always very well-mannered. He spent all that time taking me to museums. He was a little boring and had a real temper, but I would have married him if he had asked me to. He never married. He's a loner. Days and days shut up in the house and I couldn't even call him. Not because he was with other women. What he did was write in big notebooks and ask me about my life and my girlfriends' lives. Especially Maritza and Cary. We went to Alina's house together one New Year's Eve, and he spent a lot of time looking at Cary. Now I remember that

he kept my picture of her Sweet Fifteen party. (Cary gave one copy
to Alina, one to Maritza, and one to me.) But he didn't flirt with
her at all, he danced with me all night, and even put his arm
around me while Maritza was talking about those pigeon lofts.
It's true. Everytime I see them, I remember. Gray, ugly, and all the
same. I'm happier being in my little room in Old Havana and
seeing different buildings, so I can notice that people are very different too. Not like mice, pigeons, and cats. They're different
colors, yes, but basically they're all the same. If they didn't have
stains, or those colors, who could tell them apart? In Havana all
the houses are different, even if they're crumbling, while Alamar
seems like a Russian movie, I don't know. They don't even build
barbacoas there.* It was Maritza who helped me build mine. She
got the truck and even nailed the boards. It's true that she did a
lot of men's things, but to jump from there to saying that she liked
women, that's a long stretch. I don't believe it. I really don't. Just
because a friend came to live with her? And if that woman didn't
have a house, or if her husband beat her up? Maritza didn't like to
see her friends mistreated. She was very advanced. Very liberated.
That's why Alina was green with envy. She couldn't stand it that
Maritza could be happy without a man. Just staying at home,
reading, listening to nice music, classical things. If only I could
have been like her. I would have gotten a degree at night instead
of spending time in cabarets with guys who didn't know how to
respect me or be my friend.

Cary too has wasted time with a lot of people. She's run into
lots of jerks who didn't respect her. But that's different; she's fa-

---

* Alamar is a large bedroom community outside of Havana, made up
mostly of five-story concrete apartment buildings constructed according to
a single basic design. *Barbacoas* are extra rooms made by building a loft
within a single high-ceilinged room, especially common in Old Havana and
Central Havana.

mous and writes those novels. It's true that no one reads them, but that doesn't matter, once in a while she gets interviewed and she's been on TV.

cary

One afternoon at the beach, as dusk came on, Maritza was very sad. Only that day did I understand that she too could be fragile, that inside her strong body there might be a weak girl like any other. It was the first time, and the only time if I remember right, that she spoke to me about something personal.

The person she was attracted to, Maritza confessed, was in love with another. She didn't see any way that a relationship was possible, because, even if her feelings were noticed, Maritza was prepared to sacrifice herself. She wasn't going to make herself into a problem for someone she regarded so highly. She assured me that she only believed in pleasure, because love, as most people understand it, is something complex, responsible, and in a certain sense representative: a social commitment.

It was a strange conversation. I didn't dare ask who the person was. Maritza's sentiments seemed noble, but the ideas were too intricate for me. Also I felt a little afraid. The sun was setting, and conversation is transformed at that time of day. For me, they always take on a tragic tinge.

I remember: I stayed silent and, a little nervous, collected some of our things that were scattered on the rocks and began to put them in my bag. I kept myself busy that way for a while. When I looked at her again, her eyes had a devastating expression. They reflected a bitterness so great that I felt sorry for her. I thought of trying to help her, but I didn't know what was happening or understand very well what we were talking about. I ended up asking her whether the pleasure that we gave, what we gave to others, wasn't important too.

She said yes, very much. But pleasure is loaded with guilt. Many people get married—she said—believing they're in love when really they're seeking approval. Love doesn't exist, it's an invention, she repeated with the stubbornness of someone who is convinced they know the whole truth. I assured her she was wrong, that I for one did believe in love. I knew very well the difference between desiring someone and falling in love. I accepted the possibility of confusing these feelings, but to turn this confusion into an absolute seemed to me a simplification, absurd.

Then Maritza said, raising an eyebrow, that if this was how I thought, I was lost: You'll end up as a toy or something much worse, a slave.

I tried to follow Maritza, her logic. But in that moment I felt unable to grasp her message. She insisted I had to write, that writing would free me from the need to cling to some man who would represent me. You can't allow them to make you suffer, she told me. If somebody has to cry, let it be them.

I remember that after saying this she bounded up and started joking, pressing her hands against her chest and repeating herself in the affected tones of a radio announcer: Somebody has to cry, original script by Caridad Serrano, performed by Maritza Fernández.

That afternoon we parted, dying of laughter, without yet knowing that for many years we would go on having fun with her idea. Somebody has to cry, Maritza would say to me when she arrived at my house and divined my sadness over the failure of some casual relationship. Well, if somebody has to cry, let it be him, I would answer, being ironic about my sufferings and writing off the cause of my distress.

lázara

I wouldn't exchange Cary's life—what do I mean Cary's life, I woldn't even trade my own sad and insignificant one—for Alina's, her and that vain little pretty boy she got married to. He doesn't respect her. Now he doesn't even bother to hide when you run into him with some tramp at the bus stop, at a restaurant, at the most unexpected place, never with Alina but always with someone else. It seems like he's ashamed of her. Now. Because before, when Alina was young and pretty, he would introduce her boastfully: "My wife," he'd say. "Let me introduce my wife." One day, to make fun of him, Maritza said: your wife who just happens to be named Alina. He looked at her as if he wanted to swallow her and Maritza stuck out her tongue at him, right there in front of everyone. He didn't have any choice but to laugh along with the rest. But I noticed something strange, morbid. It seemed to me he wanted something with her. I could follow it in his eyes when Maritza stood up or crossed her legs. I remember that in those years when they were first married, Alina invited us to that house at the beach, and I came into the kitchen where Maritza and he were mixing the drinks. I could see it out of the corner of my eye when she pushed him away. They laughed, but she made it crystal clear: cut out the monkey business. Poor Alina in the living room, hands full with the kids, and this man fooling around with her girlfriends. Because Cary told me he made passes at her too. She asked me not to even think of telling Alina, and much less Maritza, because Maritza would call him on the carpet and throw it in his face. He's shameless. Later he didn't even want us to put Alina's name on the wreath. Maritza always said better to commit suicide than to be married to a guy like that. And now look, the one who committed suicide was her, poor thing, who was the smartest and the best of us. That's why they make up things to discredit her. That's what always happens to people who stand out. You notice that not even her friend, the one with the problem, has had the decency to show up around here. Maritza's good deeds have always been paid back that way. But I don't think she was unhappy—just the opposite. I can't explain why she did it. Cary told me something I didn't understand about the need to fulfill herself. Fulfill what, I asked. But Cary was in very bad shape. She didn't cry. It was like she couldn't do it, and I told her: It's bad for you not to cry, you have to let it out. What's it to you if Alina doesn't cry? She's very hard. But you're not, you have to cry. What we have to do now is order another wreath so that poor Maritza can have more flowers on her grave. The flowers are nice. We can ask her father—that shy man who sat in his chair and didn't even hear us when we told him our regrets—to tell us the name of the flowers so we can order another . . . Cary doesn't want me to cry, she says I'm getting hysterical. But I don't know any other way to cry. Since I was little, I've gotten these attacks of sobbing with whimpers and all. In front of Alina and her husband I made an effort to control myself. But now I can't. Why should I control myself? Maritza used to say that you have to act from your heart, and my heart is telling me to cry. I'm going to cry as much as I want and I'm going to scream too. Somebody has to cry for Maritza, somebody has to show that she wasn't this pervert they're saying she was, and so I sure am going to cry and I'm going to scream and I'm going to tell the world that she was my friend. Because somebody has to cry for her.

daniel

We buried her in a pitiless downpour and people ran to take shelter underneath the roofs of the mausoleums. When the gravediggers lowered the coffin, three of us were left: Lazarita, Caridad, and I. Cary's dry eyes reflected horror and doubt. Looking at her close up, I wondered what was left of that verdant skin, that shining body that had me lying in wait so many years, powerless but hopeful.

I kept on seeing Lazarita once in a while, just to be a little close to her. And to Maritza. Although they never looked at me. Cary always had someone, one of those men who helped her feel like everybody else. And Maritza . . . who knows? Both of them lived in worlds quite different from this one, even if they seemed to inhabit ours. To really get to know those worlds would have required great audacity, and perhaps a different sense of freedom.

I know that my comments at the funeral parlor bothered Cary. I spoke about Maritza's suicide that way to attract her attention. But she didn't remember me. She just gave me a hard stare. Then I realized that her eyes had lost their shine, that the skin around them had started to wrinkle, inevitably so.

She shifted her gaze back to the coffin: gray, absurd like the death that it hid, like Lazarita's sobbing, like the whole ritual. I knew that Cary's thoughts were headed elsewhere, to some uncertain time, perhaps, some private time—someplace where I too, together with Maritza and together with her, would have liked to be.

Until yesterday it was still possible to dream about that. Not anymore.

María Elena Llana, born 1936, is the author of the
story collections *Grillework in the Window* (1965), and
Houses of Vedado (1983) winner of that year's Critics' Prize.
She lives in Havana and is a journalist and poet as well as a
short story writer. "Japanese Daisies" is previously unpublished.

Translated by Cindy Schuster

Japanese Daisies

Siren blaring, a ship glided through the narrow channel of the bay,
almost scraping against the sea wall and the rocky platform of the
fat white Cuban cigar that was the Morro. Gertrudis sighed. She
tried to conjure up some nostalgic thought so that she might respond to the maritime wail from the bottom of her heart, but
could find none. She was happy. Then she dug around in her purse
to make sure the bill was still there. She felt a desire to toss it into
the air or the sea, but followed her original impulse to give it to
Cagliostro and made her way to the shack which served as the im-
provised meeting place for them all. It was one of those places that

could at any moment be declared clandestine, a place that sprang up from the blows of history and strove to resemble one of those small cafés that typically string their wayward rosary around port cities everywhere, although the truth is it fell short. It was as though the inevitable dilettantism of its clientele kept it more in the realm of poor man's philosophy than in that of a return to capital.

She found them all, or most of them, just as she had expected. Julio had finally left, after marrying a disabled woman from Tampico in a shameless triangulation with a travel agent, and by now Gloria must be dancing in the "Caribbean show" someplace in Cancún or Cartagena, nobody remembered which. It began with a "C," but that was irrelevant. Cagliostro and the others were there, half-dirty, half-sweaty, and pretty stewed. They were sitting around a few small coffee cups, empty already, of the kind that are crafted with lamentable simplicity and that, malevolently, lack handles.

"The fat lady has arrived," she heard. It was the best possible greeting she could hope for and she headed directly for Cagliostro, who was slumped over on the little table, with one arm extended, perhaps so as to better show off his sweaty armpit stain. From that state of greasy laxity he looked at her with his small, black, barely illuminated eyes.

"Here," she said, holding out the bill to him. Everyone exchanged rapid glances. The favored one, without abandoning his position, ordered her: "Bite it."

"What for, if it's not counterfeit?"

"So it'll be easier for you to swallow."

"You're always so original," she responded, and sat down at the next table.

Slowly, with his head spinning in foggy circles, Cagliostro began picking up the part of his body that he had deposited on the table and managed to come close to sitting up. The others continued with whatever they had been doing: one was playing with the ashtray—empty of course, that's what the floor was for—another slowly scratched his right sideburn, and a third was looking at a hole in the old, unfinished floor, as if, sooner or later, an antipode might poke its head through.

Cagliostro crossed an arm over the back of his chair and looked wearily at Gertrudis who seemed very tidy, very much the lady alone at a table as she folded the greenish rectangle lengthwise and held it out to him again.

"Take it. Just yesterday you told me you were broke."

He got up slowly and managed to connect the part of himself that lay spread out under the table with the part he had picked up from its surface. He stretched and appeared resigned when he sat down next to her, and she, with generous indifference, gave him the donation.

"Can you tell me what I'm supposed to do with this shit?"

"That's your problem. I'm just giving it to you; I have no desire to become your financial consultant."

He turned to the others: "Hear what she said? She gets a little package from Miami, probably one of the smallest, the kind they give to panhandlers over there, but only after a thousand apologies, and already she's using managerial terms."

"Ay, Calli, stop showing off! They sent me a hundred and twenty dollars."

"And a big Mickey Mouse T-shirt, a pair of tacky bedroom slippers, a few bars of Palmolive, some tubes of Colgate, and two sticks of Mum with the magic ball."

"The way things are it's pretty good, don't you think?"

"The way things are, nothing is enough."

"My understanding was that you could use a little help."

"Look, Gertrudis, if I told you about my problems, obviously what I meant was that I NEED MONEY!"

"You don't have to shout."

"I do it to show you that it's categorical, as if I were writing it in uppercase, all in caps."

"Oh, right . . . like the U.N."

Cagliostro, whose faint body odor humanized him the closer he got, looked at Jackson's somewhat distorted face and sighed. The others interrupted their esoteric soul-searching and watched as he indolently and impassively put the money away in the unclaimed upper pocket of his shirt, while shaking his head as if to say, "What's the point?"

"I'm glad you accept it. Giving it to you is a way for me to share my abundance." (Cagliostro pretended to puke.) "Perhaps it's a type of egocentricity. I, Gertrudis, am able to provide you with a glimmer of light, you, of all people!" He looked at her stone-faced: "You're so full of shit."

"No, I'm not; I'm happy. Un-be-liev-a-bly-hap-py."

The others divided up a beer and gave Gertrudis and Cagliostro a single half-filled glass. Gertrudis's bliss didn't stop her from practically snatching it from the hands of her beneficiary with a certain patronizing arrogance. But once she had the glass, she made a face and looked inside of it, searching for a fly or a worm. Cagliostro took it back and emptied it in a single gulp.

"There's light at the end of the tunnel," he said as he put down the glass, which suddenly seemed less infecto-contagious.

"Calli, ask me why I'm happy."

"Don't get me mixed up in that. It's not necessary."

It was necessary, but she resigned herself. In his seat, Cagliostro began to fashion himself into the same S shape that had twisted him up at the other table. Clearly he was getting acclimated, adapting to his new environment, and she appreciated it. He took out the pin he used in place of a shirt button that had gone on to a better life and placed it on top of one of Gertrudis's red finger-nails. Instinctively she pulled her hand away and Cagliostro pre-tended to prick the peeling wood.

"What would you think if I drove it into your nail and started the flow of . . ."

"Blood?"

". . . all the nail polish you've used ever since you were a girl."

"When I was a girl they didn't let me paint my nails."

"Right, your respectable family."

"O.K., go on with what you were saying."

"Just that what if more and more nail polish started oozing out and we kept filling bottle after bottle, how many bottles would we end up with?"

"Just imagine! There are times I've wondered, if you added up all the spoonfuls of rice, how many harvests I've managed to con-sume, on my own, in all these years."

He didn't seem to be interested in the convergence of their pre-occupations, and followed his own train of thought.

"And then, what if I prick your lips" (she brought her hand to her mouth), "and more and more lipstick begins to ooze out . . ."

"In little sticks?"

"Don't be an idiot. In cream. They'd make it into sticks later."

"Or one very long one."

"Yes!" he conceded. "It could be one really long stick and you'd never have to buy another one or ask anybody to send you one for the rest of your life. All you'd have to do would be to pass your lips over it."

It was time for her to look at him seriously. "If you really think about it, Calli, you're stuck in the perennial without realizing the period of transition we're in. What's the use of one endless lipstick, of the same color, if we open up" ("our legs," he said, but she was unfazed) "to propositions that are continually more modernized and variable?"

He responded with an ambiguous expression. He was going to answer her with something to the effect of the good thing about transitions is that when we let go of one we grab hold of another, but he took recourse in the compendium of national proverbs:

"What we are is covered with buzzard shit."

"Calli . . ."

He interrupted her brusquely: "Hey, do you know that you're the only person in the world capable of turning Calli into a nickname for Cagliostro?"

"It's just that Cagliostro is so obscure. You know, when I first met you I didn't like you because your name was such a nuisance."

"You shouldn't have changed your opinion."

"Calli," she insisted, rushing through her words so that he wouldn't be able to interrupt her, "I'm in love, I feel at peace with myself and with the world. The earth seems a more livable place, as if the harmful animals had retreated and roses were blooming."

"And long-stemmed tulips."

"I don't think they go together, but if you want . . ."

"Japanese daisies!" someone said from the other table. Gertrudis sighed, seeing her path of rosebushes trampled, but her bliss prevented her from arguing about it.

"I suppose this thing about the retreating animals is a metaphor, or at least that's your intention, right?" said Cagliostro.

"It hadn't occurred to me, but now that you mention it, it sounds good."

"It is a metaphor. The trouble is that your limited intelligence is not on a par with your natural talent."

"Ah!"

"The ones that retreat in the face of your happiness (the things you make me say!) are the little pests that cross our paths every day and go around camouflaged as people."

"It's as if you were reading my tarot," she said, amused, but he paid no attention to her and went on with his list.

"The mean-spirited, mediocre, hurtful people . . ."

"Envious, trivial, indistinguishable, ordinary people," interjected their neighbors, who were already serving themselves another beer.

"Leave some in the bottle for me," Gertrudis hastened to say.

"O.K., girl, no matter what, enjoy it while it lasts."

"It's for the rest of my life."

"All right, then, for as long as you live."

She sighed. She had made up her mind not to let Cagliostro dash her high hopes or get her down. She wasn't planning on dying ever, and especially not now that she was in love and ready to be un-be-liev-a-bly happy. The bottle came around and she reached out to take it, but he grabbed it first and took a long drink. For the first time she felt offended, hurt: wasn't that also one of those things that mean-spirited people did? Cagliostro took out a handkerchief as ragged as himself, and carefully wiped clean the mouth of the bottle. Gertrudis closed her eyes in dismay because she recognized in that hygienic gesture a desire to make amends that she couldn't reject. Her infinite weakness lay in a profound perception of the limitations of others and in the magnanimity that possessed her when faced with displays of tenderness or humility. With a smile of redeemed guilt, Cagliostro held the beer out to her:

"Drink without fear of germs."

She drank half-heartedly and her Adam's apple looked like a powdered kumquat rising and falling along her white throat, pushed up and down by the dying liquid. Cagliostro said, almost regretfully:

"You're always so fussy; you don't advance on the road to perfection."

"I don't see how being scrupulous indicates atavism . . . Besides, I'm not interested in perfection."

"But I am. Believe it or not, I've always had plans for you."

"I don't believe it," she answered, knowing that they were about to set off on one of those roads to nowhere that he had decided to take, as he once said, to amuse himself while he watched the bull from behind the fence.

"I know that as a girl you studied piano and ballet."

"Nothing special. It was part of the curriculum, like catechism and crochet."

"And I was thinking that you could do a *pas de deux*."

"With you?"

"I don't dance."

"I'm very fat."

"I can see you in a sexy little number . . ."

"With sequins?"

". . . and nothing else. Your big tits would do the *pas de deux*."

"You know I don't like vulgarities," she said, almost angry.

"Come on, girl, don't take it the wrong way. We'd get rich."

"And why would both of us get rich if I was the only one dancing?" she retorted, taking up the game again.

"Because if I don't hold your hand you'll end up in the worst sort of prostitution, without even charging. I'd be your manager, the idea man. I'd do the publicity, discuss the music, the color of the costume, the posters and the lighting."

"You're contradicting yourself," she said slowly and vengefully. "You're bent on your image of failure in the midst of collapse and, even though you say you don't trust changes, you engage in lucrative flirtations."

"Yeah, but only about a seedy dump, the place for fallen angels."

"Your quality's slipping. Now you're turning phrases."

"We could call it the Alma Mater," he said, inspired, "and it would be an effort to prevent any more talent-drain. We have the unfortunate loss of Gloria and Julio, very close to us, don't we? Throughout the Caribbean basin they ask for our historian whores and our butt-fucking philologists . . . I wonder if they take their diplomas with them, or if they leave them hanging so that their mothers, between waiting in line after line and sitting through one blackout after another, can feel some smoldering orgasmic remains."

"I'm not going to argue with you."

"That's your Puritanism. If I were to say the same thing with fancy references, you'd accept it."

"What I don't accept is the generalization; don't twist my words. If it were like that I'd go hustling tourists too."

He let out a truly impudent guffaw. And the others did the same, spontaneously, not just to ingratiate themselves with him. Gertrudis adopted a tiresomely didactic tone:

"There's nothing exclusive about sex. If there are those who seek out starving black women, why can't there be those who get turned on by a well-bathed fat woman? I can play Mommy for them, with dental floss and a Victorian bonnet."

"You're not lacking in imagination," ventured Cagliostro.

"It would be a success given the quality of the clientele, because ambitious vendors are coming to the street market to deal in toothbrushes and sixty-watt light bulbs under the guise of being foreign businessmen . . . the same undercurrent that's brought us to the edge of the drain pulls them too."

"The drainpipes and the toilets haven't been working for a long time, you know that," he said, trying to open an umbrella in the middle of the rainstorm, but instead inciting her further.

"We had to flush then with buckets of water. The buckets weren't cheap either, and half the time there wasn't even any water. It's always been like that, it's true, but we didn't see it, because we've been victims of this damn virus which is endemic in some people."

"AIDS?" he teased.

"Dreams!" she concluded, defying the ridicule that her sentimentality might provoke. But they all kept quiet. Then, as if there were nothing more to say, she took out her compact and began struggling to frame her fat face in the little mirror. She powdered her nose, took her lipstick, smeared it properly over her lips and, after making a few faces in order to distribute the color evenly, put it away again. She was obviously getting ready to leave, but Cagliostro held her by the wrist.

"What's his name?"

"It doesn't matter anymore."

"It does matter, damn it," he said, trying to recover his authority. "If you've finally met a guy you like and, on top of that, they send you little packages from Miami, you deserve some recognition, don't you?"

"What for?"

"For your ability to maintain a certain equilibrium."

"It was just luck, there's no merit in it . . . Could you be any luckier than a whale walking a tightrope?"

"You agree with me. Enviable capacity for equilibrium."

And he insisted, venturing to put his hand on hers, which was already resting on her purse, ready to take flight:

"I'm not going to let you leave without at least telling me his name."

Once again she let herself be won over by condescension at this sign of repentance from Cagliostro who, to top it off, ordered a big round of beer for everyone, undoubtedly to be paid for with that little scrap of green which he was incapable of dedicating to more important things: another variant of his ability to get side-tracked. A ship blared and as if by tacit agreement nobody bothered to watch it thread its way through the neck of the harbor in search of the open sea.

They all drank. Gertrudis had the pleasure of a bottle all to herself and as she sipped delightedly, she heard again:

"What's his name?"

Cagliostro's insistence brought her back to her natural trusting self. She allowed love to soften her words and with a half-smile confessed:

"Narciso."

Any trace of tension evaporated with the unanimous guffaw that burst out from the other table. Cagliostro took the twenty dollars out of his pocket and made a gesture to give them back to her with an expression that showed he knew the situation was hopeless.

"Here, take it, I don't like to swindle anybody."

All her hopes of leaving were dashed and she remained glued to the chair, with both hands on her purse, as if she were listening to a new administrative admonition. The others also took an interest in Cagliostro's attitude, which put off the final verdict. Adopting the role of redeemer, he was oblivious to Gertrudis's silent plea, applying the maxim that he who really loves you will make you cry. Suddenly, she seemed to have a revelation and dared to tell him:

"But there's no danger. He's not at all conceited and he doesn't even look at himself in puddles."

Cagliostro fixed small, hard, and severe eyes on her. Everyone once again waited on his words, which were not open to appeal:

"With a name like that he's not going anywhere."

Gertrudis's anguish diminished, surrendering to a childlike happiness that gave her back the right to enjoy life:

"That doesn't matter! I call him Tamerlane! I swear I've always called him Tamerlane, my little Tamerlane." Cagliostro pursed his lips, shook his head a little, and looked at her. Once again the juggling of words, the power to free them from their strict dictionary definition in order to let them flow freely until they lent even catastrophe the *new look* of promise . . . Yes, without doubt he discerned a hope, but he didn't dare take it seriously. Since she insisted with her overflowing happiness, he put the money back in his pocket and simply said, putting all the responsibility on her:

"If you think so . . ."

At the next table the anticipation gave way and each of them went back to their own self-absorption, without noticing that a slight, flexible guy was sticking his head out of the hole in the floor. Upon verifying that his presence attracted no interest, the antipode supported himself as best he could on the rim and catapulted himself outside. He still hesitated to perform the grand circus finale, but he could tell that no one here would bat an eye. So he sat down with the others and, without pausing to see whether or not the glass was clean, parsimoniously began to drink the few drops of beer with which they welcomed him.

Josefina de Diego was born in 1951 into a family of Cuban writers. She lives in Havana where she is an economist by profession. Her first book of stories, *Grandfather's Kingdom*, was published in Mexico in 1993. "Internal Monologue on a Corner in Havana" (1996) is previously unpublished.

Translated by Dick Cluster

Internal Monologue on a Corner in Havana

God, I'm dying for a cigarette! If only my pension got me through the month, I wouldn't have to sell my rationed smokes. But a peso apiece, that's not bad, with that I can buy a little rice and a head of garlic every now and then. You can't do much on eighty pesos a month. Who would have thought that after twenty-plus years of work and with a university degree, I'd have to stand here on this corner selling my monthly cigarettes? And surreptitiously, because there's no way I'm getting caught in this "profit-oriented activity," as they say these days—without paying the tax on it I'd be in jail for sure. And how I love to smoke! But, in truth, I can't complain. This corner is quite entertaining, everybody's mixed up in something, more or less the same as me. Really it's a prime spot: the Farmers' Market and two kiosks of CADECA, the Houses of Hard-Currency Exchange. Such an ugly acronym, they really outdid themselves this time. There are other terrible, historic ones, like CONACA or ECOA, but this is one of the worst. Sometimes I miss potential customers because I'm amusing myself by people-watching. It's comical, almost musical. You hear, "psst, psst, *change money*, listen, exchange," all the time, like a timid hawker's chant. Or else the old man who sidles up so mysteriously and tells you "I fix gas stoves" and keeps walking, and you don't know whether you really heard it or you imagined it all. The other day a lady let loose a really hair-raising yell because she thought the old guy was a thief, and then there was a hell of a fuss. The old man didn't show his face in the market for about a week. I could smoke this cigarette right now. God, how hard it is to quit! If it hadn't been for this illness, I'd still be working and things wouldn't be so tough. When they told me they were retiring me on eighty pesos for "total incapacity to work," I almost had a fit. What an absurd law, since when you get sick is when you have to spend the most. But all the letters I sent, complaining, didn't do a bit of good. That's the law. And eighty pesos, at the official rate, that's less than four dollars. So therefore: Improvise! Once in a while somebody with dollars drops a coin or two, which helps my budget out. The one who's even worse off than me is the guy who sells plastic bags from the *shopping*,* for a peso. This truly is illegal, more illegal than what I do, because at least I bought my little

---

* The *shopping*, pronounced "choppin," is Cuban slang for the network of hard-currency (dollar) stores, now accessible to Cubans and foreigners alike. The nickname probably comes from the bilingual ad for one such chain: *compras fáciles,* "easy shopping."

cigarettes myself, but those bags, where did he get them from? Whenever I can, I warn him of possible inspectors. We have a kind of unofficial union of "you scratch my back and I'll scratch yours." We're all here for the same reason, trying to get by without hurting anybody much. In fact, it doesn't seem to me we're hurting anyone at all, but I can understand how the Government can't allow it. If everybody were like us—but no, people are too much, if you give them an inch they'll take a mile and they'll end up robbing you with machine guns like in American films. Boy, how I miss my TV! A few days ago it broke on me and now I can't even watch the soaps. Luckily just the picture went out, so at least you can hear it. 'Cause getting it fixed, forget it, it's Japanese, Sanyo, and the repairman charges in dollars. At least my nephew is an electronic technician and soon he'll be back from a mobilization in the countryside—he went with the university. The mobilizations of the sixties and seventies, they were fun. Or at least that's how I remember them. Maybe it's just the "good old days" always seeming better, I don't know. I always thought they weren't very productive, especially the Sunday morning ones. "The important thing is attitude, *compañera*," they told me when I tried to demonstrate to the leader in question that between gas, snack, depreciation on the truck tires, oil, et cetera, the cost was greater than any possible income. "Professional vices," he told me. "Be optimistic. You economists think too much." In those days to buy a pack of cigarettes over and above the ration was just a peso and sixty centavos—shocking—and now they charge ten. What I'd love to do would be to buy a jar of that coconut sweet from the guy across the way there, but for a dollar? That's what I get for a whole pack of loose cigarettes, no way. Maybe later on, if I get some "reinforcements" from my sister who lives in Venezuela. Every now and then along come a few dollars that I sure can use. If I sell all these cigarettes I'm going to treat myself to a paper cone full of banana chips, for two pesos, two cigarettes, that's not bad. You can't always live in austerity, no sir, because "Life is a Dream," as my high school literature teacher always used to say. Such a good teacher! He made us learn a few things by heart, to improve our vocabularies he said. I never thought I'd come to understand so perfectly the part about "when he turned his head/he found his answer on viewing/that another wise man was chewing/his discarded crust of bread." Around here there are tons of those wise men. But the one who's really worse off than me is the one who picks through the garbage dumpster in front of my house. The poor man, he doesn't know there's never anything of value in there—I give it a quick look every day. He ought to go to one by some embassy or near the hotels. Although it's not so easy, because those dumpsters have got their proprietors by now. If I don't sell these cigarettes soon, I'm leaving, because it looks like Noah's Flood is about to hit. And I'll end up with no banana chips. Yesterday one of my neighbors, in the building across the street, put a sign up on his porch: "Plumber—house calls." He must be dimwitted, how else can he fix plumbing except by making house calls? There's a lot of nuttiness, people are posting all kinds of signs, hilarious ones. Not to mention the names of the *paladares.** Cubans have a certain nostalgia for small businesses and for advertisements different from the official ones, which sometimes makes you want to cry: "The Delights of Eden," right, and what you see are three little tables with a few homemade tablecloths. But clean, and with pleasant staff. I worked in one, and things were going really well, but then it got closed down and I

---

* *Paladares*, literally "palates," are small family-run restaurants in people's homes. The popular term comes from the name of a fast-food chain started by a character in a Brazilian soap opera shown on Cuban TV.

was in the street again. Now it's started pouring, ugh, what do I do now? Smoke the cigarette and not buy the chips? A dilemma worse than Hamlet's! How would it go in my case, teacher? "To smoke or to eat, that is the question." That would be funny if it weren't the truth, and if weren't for the fact that this is me instead of some latter-day tropical Hamlet. Better I should take the cigarette home and, if there's gas, make a little coffee and have my smoke. As they say in that charming English movie, "Life isn't perfect and besides, it's short." Tomorrow's another day. Who knows, maybe a few bucks from my sister will turn up.

Nancy Alonso, born 1949, is a physiology professor in Havana. Her first book of stories, *Throw the First Stone*, won honorable mention in the annual contest of the Cuban National Union of Writers and Artists in 1995. "A Tooth for a Tooth" appeared in the anthology *Pillars of Salt* (1996).

Translated by Dick Cluster

Nancy Alonso

A Tooth for a Tooth

With difficulty, Pepe Cruz managed to get off the bus which took him from work to home. A wave of humanity had followed him on, without much caring that they were leaving their predecessors trapped. Hurrying, nearly running, he retraced the route to the corner and then turned left. It was a few minutes before seven, when the supermarket would close, and Pepe Cruz was hoping to buy eggs—assuming the shipment expected for several days had now arrived. He peeked through the store window, and all his dreams dissolved. Below the battered sign reading "meat products," the counter was deserted—the counter for distributing eggs, which were meat in an embryonic state.

Downhearted, he slowly walked away from the store. The final days of Pepe Cruz's month had become a torment, as they had for millions of Cubans. The monthly quota assigned by the food supply book barely covered the needs of the first twenty days. What peculiarities of language, Pepe Cruz thought: since the coupon book had been established more than thirty years ago (and who then would have said that now, nearing the end of the century and millennium, it would still be around?), it had always been called the *supply book*, never *ration book* as it had been called in Europe during the world wars. This was the eternal spirit of optimism, the philosophy that saw a glass of water as never half empty, always half full.

Pepe Cruz remembered the golden age when there had been another market parallel to the rationed one. You could buy food and clothes at prices a little higher but accessible to the majority of family budgets nonetheless. That was at the end of the seventies and through most of the eighties. Those stores full of merchandise from the socialist countries (or just *the countries* for short): Chinese hot dogs and peaches, Vietnamese rice chips, Bulgarian pickled cucumbers and sweet conserves, Czech stuffed cabbage, German sausage, Soviet canned meat and powdered milk, Polish sauces, Albanian and Hungarian wines. What a Republic that was! Pepe Cruz never understood those who left for the United States in that era. Nonetheless, between then and now things had changed plenty. Now only the black market and the dollar stores were well-supplied. Neither of those was accessible to a university professor like himself, without any help from relatives abroad.

With the public street lights shut off, the darkness of the street where Pepe Cruz lived made it hard to avoid the holes in the sidewalk, barely visible in the faint light from some of the homes. The stench of the neighborhood was unmistakable: to the joy of rodents and cockroaches, another day without garbage collection would make six. As if these calamities in the life of Pepe Cruz weren't enough, his wife Elena was in the interior of the country on a work-related trip, and he had to take care of all the domestic problems, among which was making dinner while having hardly anything to make it from.

Since there was no light in the doorway of his house, he knew that Jorgito, his fourteen-year-old son, hadn't yet come home from school. Jorgito always came in turning on lights, radio, tape recorder, fans, everything, including his father's anger. That is, if there was electricity, of course. Pepe Cruz felt for his key and managed to introduce it into the keyhole without great trouble. For more than half his life, he'd gone through the same motion almost daily, so why would he need light to do that? He could reach the kitchen without turning on a single lamp along the route through the living-dining room and the hallway off of which the bedrooms lay. In this fashion he compensated for Jorgito's wastefulness.

Opening the refrigerator, Pepe Cruz glanced at the scarce provisions: a little white rice and black beans saved from the day before, and a chunk of cabbage. That was all. At least there was still gas to heat up the food, he consoled himself while putting the pots of rice and beans over a low flame. He decided he would make the salad after his shower, taking advantage of the fact that there was still running water so he could avoid the hated bucket and can. For three years now, the country had been living like this, trying to take advantage of every opportunity: take advantage of the fact that there's water, and bathe; take advantage of the fact that the gas came on, and cook; take advantage of the fact that there's current, and iron; take advantage of the fact that the eggs showed up, and eat protein. It didn't matter when the opportunity appeared, you had to take advantage of it then. With even the most simple project impossible to carry out, everything was provisional in a most crushing way.

Nervously, fearing a blackout or the loss of running water in the shower, Pepe Cruz went to his room for a change of underwear and his pajamas. He hurriedly took off his shirt, shoes, and socks, and put a pair of half-destroyed sandals on his feet. He finished undressing in the bathroom, and felt somewhat comforted when a forceful stream of water covered his head and the cold liquid flowed over him into every hidden corner of his body. It was an ineffable moment, as if the shower were a baptism and the holy water would wash away all the annoyances of his day, carrying off the slights, the pointless paperwork, and the aggressiveness he'd had to confront, cleaning him of the shoving in the bus and the bad smells of the street, purging him of despair and discouragement, purifying him until he felt nearly immaculate.

Pepe Cruz was still enjoying the watery exorcism when he heard the typical slamming of the door that meant Jorgito was home. Right away he heard his son calling, "Is that you, old man?"

"Either it's me or it's the seven-thirty burglar taking a shower," answered Pepe Cruz, a bit annoyed by the noisy arrival of his son, which would pull him away from the escape of the shower. Besides, he couldn't stand being called *old man* when he was barely forty, but Jorge insisted on referring to him that way.

"Don't play games, old man, I'm starving to death and not interested in jokes," Jorgito shot back, and added right away, "What is there to eat?"

Pepe Cruz turned off the water and began to rub the washcloth with a minuscule piece of soap, the only piece left, which was thanks to the gift of a student, because he couldn't even remember the last time there'd been soap offered on the coupon book. He took a breath before answering his son:

"What you see on the stove, plus a little cabbage salad. The eggs didn't come in at the store."

"Damn, that's no good." After yelling this, Jorgito went off to the living-dining room to turn on the radio at full blast. From there he shouted again, but Pepe Cruz couldn't make it out.

"I can't hear you over that music, Jorgito!"

A few seconds later, Pepe Cruz heard his son's muted voice, and imagined him with his mouth up against the crack of the bathroom door, making faces the way he did when he thought nobody could see.

"There was a guy here to see you this morning, some Alejandro Quesada or something like that, I'm not sure."

"Who did you say was here to see me?" Pepe Cruz asked, while he soaped his face with his eyes shut tight. He didn't know anybody by that name.

"Alejandro Quesada. No, wait, it was Armando de Quesada," Jorgito corrected himself, now sure of the visitor's name.

"Armando de Quesada!" Pepe Cruz exclaimed, astonished. The surprise of this unexpected news opened his eyes wide, and they began burning terribly as soon as they filled with soap. He turned on the faucet and threw water on his face, thinking that he knew Armando de Quesada very well.

"That's what he said his name was, I'm sure of it. Oh, he left you a package, a present. Didn't you see it on the table?"

"No, I didn't see it," said Pepe Cruz. "Did he give you any message for me? Did he say whether he would come back?"

"The only thing he said was his name and that I should give you this present from him. That's all."

Pepe Cruz didn't continue the conversation with Jorgito. He

dove into the neglected crevices of his memory to dust off the image of Armando de Quesada. Or, really, the various images of Armando, Mandy for his close associates, stored away since the time when they'd been friends.

Mandy and he had met in high school; it would have been around 1965. Until 1980, when that terrible situation occurred, they'd maintained a relationship which, though not intimate, was close enough. They studied in different fields but within the same faculty, the faculty of sciences of the University of Havana. When they'd graduated, they'd both stayed on to work as professors in their respective departments, separated by less than a hundred yards within the precincts of the academy. Therefore they'd seen each other often. They would meet in the snack bar during break time, in the dining hall at lunch time, and in countless faculty meetings too. At the time the problem happened, Mandy had been giving math classes in the physics department, Pepe Cruz's department, which was another thing that had maintained the ties between the two.

Pepe Cruz found he was scrubbing the same part of his arm again and again. He was so absorbed in his memories that he had no idea how much time had gone by. He finished washing in a hurry so he could see Mandy's present. With the quantity of needs he'd accumulated, almost anything would seem good to Pepe Cruz. A few bars of soap, for instance, to lighten his worry about the sliver that was disappearing between his hands along with any hope of replacing it. Maybe, he thought, Mandy had left a note, a letter, something that would tell him the reason for this morning's visit after so many years of absence—and what an irony it would be, one of life's ironies, if Mandy now offered a helping hand to overcome the shortages plaguing his family and himself. The fact of Mandy's having come to see him and having brought him a present meant one of two things: either Mandy hadn't seen him on that horrible day, or Mandy had been able to rationalize it and, to some degree, forgive him. In any case, Mandy wanted to see him, to be in communication, and this cheered Pepe Cruz, who'd spent years trying to forget the events that had separated them. Mandy had always been very helpful to Pepe Cruz, and to say anything else would have been a lie.

While drying himself off, Pepe Cruz reviewed Mandy's personality traits. He was an intelligent fellow, organized and capable in his profession. Perhaps for this reason, he'd been elected a member of the trade union bureau of the faculty, even though Mandy had never been a barrel of laughs, was something of a despot with the students, and was also, some said, capable of stabbing anyone in the back. An opportunist of the worst order, according to Abel, also a coworker of the old guard. Pepe Cruz wondered whether Mandy might have gone to Abel's house now, and what Abel would say about all this. He'd never been able to guess Abel's reactions, always so different from those of the rest of the group. For instance, the day of the events, Abel did what nobody could have predicted. He kept on teaching his class on the second floor of the physics building, imperturbably, without changing the inflection of his voice as he said, "I'm not calling off my lecture to go anywhere; the rest of you can do what you think fit." After all these years, Pepe Cruz still couldn't believe Abel's boldness. He decided to call him on the phone as soon as he'd opened Mandy's present.

Pepe Cruz dried himself hurriedly and didn't even put on his underwear. He left the bathroom with the towel wrapped around his waist and water still dripping from his hair. He headed for the living-dining room where Jorgito was perched on the sofa in the evident position of a crow waiting to pounce on his food. Crow was about all they'd both have to eat tomorrow if the blessed eggs didn't arrive at the store.

"Look, old man, here's the package," Jorgito said while pointing in the direction of the table.

Pepe Cruz saw a rectangular box, covered with very handsome wrapping paper, the kind printed in very bright colors which he hadn't seen in quite a long time and couldn't have even imagined now. As he'd expected, he found a small envelope stuck to the package, alongside a flower made of snippets of pink cloth. Pepe Cruz hurried to read the note written in Mandy's unmistakable hand: "Pepe: Please accept this modest gift. I know how much you need it, in more ways than one. Accept it as a tribute to my good memory. Armando de Quesada (Mandy)." Pepe Cruz felt a bit embarrassed and also quite moved by Mandy's note. He thought again about the turns life takes: friendship is friendship, whatever the disagreements in between.

"Who's this Armando de Quesada, old man?" Jorgito's question drew him out of his meditation.

"He's Mandy, an old friend," answered Pepe Cruz in a cheerful tone. "It's a long story, Jorgito, and we're both too hungry to talk about it now."

The fact was, Pepe Cruz didn't dare to tell his son the details of the break with Mandy. It would be very hard for Jorgito to understand his father's conduct in an era before he was even born. It was in 1980. Elena had been three months pregnant when the whole mess took place. Pepe Cruz remembered perfectly how the threads of the story had begun to interweave. One day Mandy had arrived at the physics department to run a "lightning meeting," which meant one called on the spot. He, better than anyone, could put together a speech with all the union rhetoric of the era at the drop of a hat.

"Okay, comrades," Mandy had begun his address, "our revolutionary government has decided to open the port of Mariel so that persons from the United States can come collect all the Cuban citizens who want to leave. But before leaving Cuba, they must show immigration authorities an entitling document that demonstrates they've requested dismissal from their place of study or work. That means that we'll know who intends to abandon the country, and it allows us to give them a lively response. In the presence of those citizens, we'll carry out acts of political reaffirmation of the revolutionary spirit of workers, students, and the people in general, and in the process we can also demonstrate our repugnance toward the treason of those who desert."

Thus Mandy had announced, with all that rhetoric, what later became known as "acts of repudiation."

"Old man, do you smell that, the beans are burning!" Jorgito shouted. Pepe Cruz snapped out of his memories and ran into the kitchen followed by his son. He turned off the flame and uncovered the pot to reveal the beans, almost dry.

"Do you think they can be saved, old man?"

"Luckily, yes, they're not beyond repair," affirmed Pepe Cruz with relief, as he began to pour water on the smoking beans. "Everything in life has a solution, Jorgito, everything but death, as my grandmother used to say. Look at this—look at Mandy after so much time, when I didn't have the faintest idea I'd ever see him again, and here he shows up with a gift."

"You still haven't told me what this Mandy brought," Jorgito complained.

"Didn't you see that I had to put the package down to take care of the food? I can't be in the Mass and the procession at the same time," argued Pepe Cruz while he put the beans back on the heat. "Let the rice sit and we'll fix up the beans a little. Then we'll open the package." After a pause, he repeated the old saying. "Yes, it's hard being in the Mass and the procession at the same time."

Chance, or maybe fate, had decreed that neither Abel nor he had been in the building when the first acts of repudiation were organized. In those turbulent days, the two of them had been sent to do an evaluation in the province of Camagüey, much to the delight of Pepe Cruz. When they got back, their coworkers had filled them in on what they'd missed. Especially, on Mandy's active and noteworthy participation at the head of several acts of repudiation. As always, he had shown himself very enthusiastic when the time came to harass and dominate those whom he considered his enemies.

"What's bothering you, old man? You look half-cracked, stirring the beans and staring at the bottom of the pot."

"Show me some respect, Jorgito. I've already told you not to call me 'old man.' I'm seeing to it that these beans don't stick to the pot again, so we can finally sit down and eat." Pepe Cruz argued back, though he knew his son was right. Mandy's reappearance in his life, and with it the ghosts of the past assaulting the present, was proving to be a real shock. Similar to that other shock, the one he'd experienced when someone told him something that seemed inconceivable. Right away he'd called Abel on the telephone to share the news, and now Pepe Cruz could recall the conversation perfectly, as if fifteen years hadn't gone by.

"Abel, it's me, Pepe Cruz. You're not going to believe me. Are you sitting down?"

"Yes, Pepe, tell me."

"Guess who requested dismissal to go to the United States?"

"Mandy."

"You already heard?"

"No, but I can imagine it."

That was Abel. And, being the way he was, he had stayed away from the most sensational act of repudiation put on by the workers and students of the faculty of sciences, while Pepe Cruz, as a member of that crowd, had shakily approached Mandy's home. He had to go, what choice was there? On the one hand, if anybody deserved repudiation, it was Mandy, so shameless, after presenting himself as the most gung-ho of all; on the other hand, he was afraid of the consequences of refusing, because they could think that he too wanted to leave or that he was supporting his friend Mandy. Despite all that, Abel didn't participate, and he continued to be a university professor. When the crowd arrived across from Mandy's place the shouts and insults began, and Pepe Cruz tried to straggle behind so as to be with god and the devil at once.

"Old man, will you let me open the package?" asked Jorgito from the living-dining room.

"Yes," Pepe Cruz answered mechanically while he served the supper onto plates and continued to conjure up the first act of repudiation of his life. Others had followed, and it hadn't been so bad, one gets accustomed to everything—even to witnessing, now, this exodus of rafters seen off by relatives and friends as if it were nothing at all.

He couldn't remember who threw the first stone against Mandy's house and broke a pane of glass in one of the windows. Nor could he say precisely where the boxes of eggs came from, nor when the crowd began to throw them so that they splattered against the front door, against the walls. Although he could call to mind, clearly, the sound of eggs exploding—plaf! plaf!—and the appearance of the whites and yolks sliding stickily along the plaster and wood, the shells scattered on the ground, he never knew who had said to him, "What are you waiting for, Pepe Cruz, why don't you start throwing eggs at Mandy? Or don't you have what it takes?" Nor who had put a full box of eggs in his hands, warning or ordering him to participate as more than a mere spectator. At that moment, Pepe Cruz had thought that he was effectively a coward: he had no balls, because if he'd had any he would have refused to take part. Beginning to throw eggs, he felt ashamed to see himself and to be seen in this act of barbarism. But little by little he felt impelled by an internal force, a force of vindication. Mandy had fooled them, Mandy had swindled them. He deserved to have his house messed up a little, his house more and more stained by spitefully thrown eggs, if he was going to the U.S. Furthermore, Pepe Cruz, who was staying, was not inclined to expose himself to what could happen if he refused to repudiate Mandy. Refused like Abel, who said that acts of this type dishonored the victimizers more than the victims.

"Old man, we're saved, look at the present your pal Mandy gave you!" Jorgito came into the kitchen and showed his father the contents of the box. "Eggs! This will save the day, old man."

Pepe Cruz looked inside the box and then at his son, with an expression Jorgito couldn't decipher at all. He walked slowly over to the telephone and dialed a number. After a few seconds, Jorgito heard him say in a very tired voice: "Abel, it's me, Pepe Cruz. Guess who came from the U.S."

Mylene Fernández Pintado was born in 1963. Her first short story, "Anhedonia (A Story in Two Women)," won an honorable mention in the contest of *La Gaceta de Cuba* in 1994, and was published in the Cuban anthology *Pillars of Salt* in 1996. Fernández lives in Havana.

Translated by Dick Cluster

Anhedonia

(A Story in Two Women)

> Heard melodies are sweet,
> but those unheard
> are sweeter
> Keats
> "Ode on a Grecian Urn"

Sabina is predictable. Sabina's future was predictable in the past, or, that is, Sabina's present was predictable when the past was the present. Oh, what a mess!

Everybody respected her. She started games and finished them, she made fun of people and things with cruel, delicious wit, and nobody ever made jokes at her expense. Being her friend was like having a gold credit card: those who owe are delighted to pay. That's how it was when she needed something. Every one of us was disposed to offer it to her, and especially to offer company, to lend an ear to her words, to put a hand in hers.

Why did she choose me? I admired her in secret: her sureness, her wisdom, her spark, her world, but I was too timid to demand her attention so I went on living my life, watching her from afar without daring to approach her, and then it happened. She was in front of the class doing impressions of everyone, with considerable success, and when she got to me she said, "No, not you, you're too ordinary." The next thing I knew, she'd moved her books to my table and from then on she sat next to me anyplace where two people could fit. Even on my wedding day, when she drew up her chair alongside the two already in position, and sat herself down.

There she is, in this photo and in all the others, with her boyish haircut, her thin lips, and her face that said whatever was happening could happen because it had her consent. In a way, that was her: she used to say that chance took only the lazy and the stupid by surprise. She said her life was a script she wrote and, of course, it was a good script in which nothing was missing and nothing was in excess. Yes, she would allow me to get married, but that was all—allow, which means let happen, not to do oneself. To her, Sergio seemed unworthy of me—"he's not much, and you're so brilliant"—but okay, it was my caprice and therefore could be tolerated. But no more than that. She danced the whole night and then took off with my parents' best friend, who had come with his wife and kids, and she didn't give him back until a week later, minus briefcase, calendar, business cards, and fountain pen. The poor man went into an identity crisis. His wife put him in the back room of the house and made him answer the phone and beg favors for everyone else. Then he died. It was said that he'd been ill. I know Sabina made him sick and made him dependent. She supplied him with great doses of happiness, and when she cut him off he couldn't endure. But I could. I'm a survivor, and a worthy one; after my wedding day I didn't see her again until today.

Seven years is a long time, even if all I've done with it is to have a job in which I'm intelligent and gray like a nerve cell and to have my son whom I enchant because I'm the only mother he's got. If he had two mothers, I'd be in second place. Every day is the same, isn't it? Today I argue with my boss, tomorrow I fix it up, and the next day Victor Manuel gets sick. (I named my son after the Spanish singer of "I Only Think of You," after the painter of tropical gypsies, and after a drunk and fantasy-prone neighbor whose wife and daughter are harpies with whom he acts like Don Quijote facing the windmills, without a chance. But this man bears up and I admire him for that.)

A baby is an abrupt change in your life. My début as a mother was traumatic. After going through the whole day disheveled, with rough hands and dull eyes, I went to bed for the night thinking that maybe tomorrow would be different. It never was. It took me a long time to realize that true motherhood means you enjoy all this in a loving and magnanimous fashion, and on balance you feel happy as a result. But my capacity for resignation was less than the average. At times I'd be holding Victor and catch myself thinking about something else instead of teaching him to say "Mama" and "Dada." What would I have been like without Sergio and Victor? Like Sabina. Independent, unique, without commitments of time or sentiment; as if Mephistopheles had given a mature woman all the time in the world for herself. In exchange for what?

Sabina was professionally explosive. Whatever she did showed off her IQ. She liked speaking her strange language full of obscure literary quotes for her own consumption (and mine). I was a kind of messenger between her and the rest of the mere mortals who were unacquainted with Anatole France and failed to listen to Wagner. I can imagine her today: sure, efficient, tough, and exquisitely professional. A complete executive. Without my seeing her, she kept leaving me crumbs to show her path. A book published, a TV appearance, an interview in a monthly magazine, studies abroad, and many mutual friends who commented on her success like something written in the stars. While I, sometimes I surprise myself in my stupid everydayness and my mediocre job, where everybody thinks I'm efficient but it doesn't get me anywhere, except that I don't have to exert myself to get things done. I'm a perfect doer who never initiates. Sabina was always full of ideas, and her work life is what I always imagined. Working meals, telex, fax, secretary, driver, influence; in sum, an adult who does serious work.

She hasn't married. I know this doesn't bother her. She can have all the lovers she wants. And drop them without the slightest scruple. Her opinion of the opposite sex can't have changed with the years. As she used to say, every moment, whether a vacation or a semester, should have an associated name and face—but that's all.

Sabina was superior to all the boys. She flirted a little, made fun of them, didn't take them seriously. She had a thousand romances which began and ended without her feeling it. She lived her adolescence with the perspective of maturity, as if a woman of thirty were given the opportunity to be fifteen again. She knew this was not a stage of important decisions. It was as if she were recopying the draft of this period after correcting and improving it, living those years with the carefree lack of inhibition one wishes to have lived them with, now that it's too late. Adolescence is heavy, contrary to what everyone says. Every step and every attitude seems irreversible, definitive, as if there's no going back. We suffer with the imminence of every action. We need help but are always alone with ourselves.

Sabina already knew better. No boy was included in her future, she didn't care what anyone thought. Someone had revealed to her what she'd be like when she grew up, and in the meantime she was enjoying herself the way a student enjoys the vacation before a difficult year.

Her relationship with Sergio was like that, trivial and joking. She didn't take him seriously. Our engagement surprised her quite a bit, but she was a kind of guardian of our happiness. I almost think she came to the wedding just to see the evidence of my folly. I wouldn't label it that way. I think I did with Sergio what I've done with everything else: I let myself be taken, loved, made pregnant, all without an effort, carried along by my congenital comfort.

It's as if I haven't lived my life, but lent my person so that others could place it in the necessary spots for them to live theirs. Victor's mother, Sergio's wife. I still can't identify the moment in which Sergio stopped loving me and adopted me instead. It must have happened slowly, without my noticing. I'm slow and impassive like phlegm; he's flowing and active like blood. Little by little I turned things over to him. It was more comfortable, because he had energy enough for two and this way I never ran the risk of making mistakes. He did. Now it's too late to recover control of our common life. I can't even recover control of my own. Sergio knows everything—what's good for me, for Victor, for the house, my work, my family, my friends, my hobbies. Sometimes (to be truthful, it's not often) we argue. When I say *argue* I'm not talking about each of us putting forward our different points of view so we can confront them rationally, but rather about hysterical outbursts provoked by the accumulation of so many problems with no way out. Then I don't speak to him for three days because he took too long to answer the telephone. I'm the only one who knows that this reaction is a concentrated response to three months of grievances. Since I don't say so, Sergio lives on convinced that I'm a neurotic with extraordinary responses to insignificant things about which, furthermore, I'm always wrong.

Most of the time I'm too tired to argue, and so I let him live for both of us. My revenge is of a different type: my soul isn't married to anyone, and I'd do anything for him except surrender my stubborn spirit of singleness. I'll take the consequence, a marriage in which nothing is going on behind the scenes. For everyone else, we're a witty couple and a harmonious case of opposites attract. But a performance and its daily rehearsal are miles apart.

Others see our life as a series of photos or vignettes—or, to speak in terms of movement, a series of scenes. These short intervals allow people who don't live with us to draw conclusions about what our life is like. It's not the same if we run into an acquaintance while leaving the theater as it is in line at the pharmacy, even if we've gone to the theater as an alternative to suicide and to the pharmacy to buy gravinol because we're going on a trip and always get nauseous when we fly. These explanations don't form part of the photograph, of the instant in which we are sharing information. Of course, people attach past and future to their pictures, and so try to vitiate the image which they've involuntarily offered, by adding stories of causes and consequences, premises and perspectives; but these footnotes never matter as much as the fact of having been taken by surprise in a moment of their lives.

I remember a night when Sergio and I went to eat at a fancy restaurant. It was one of those nights which seem to close a chapter in one's life. His father had lent him the car, I'd had my hair cut the day before, we were elegant as could be, and the next day we were going to the beach for vacation. At the restaurant we met an acquaintance who took that image of material and spiritual welfare away with him. Yet as soon as we left, the car broke down. When I went to get help, I lost my purse. Sergio sprained something trying to push the car, and when we got home at dawn, drenched with sweat and starving, there had been a call about a mixup in the reservations which put the whole vacation in jeopardy. By way of contrast, our acquaintance, with his barely acceptable attire, was the director of a comedy group which soon received an offer of work abroad where they were a tremendous success.

When Sabina and I ran into each other after so many years, my vignette was among the worst imaginable. It was as if I had a seal stamped on my forehead that classified me: mediocre, bored, and resigned, a trilogy no one could envy at all.

The night before, Victor had run a high fever. Sergio and I took advantage of the wee hours we spent watching over his bed to say to each other all the disagreeable things that fear, exhaustion, and remorse can generate. We repeated over and over again our interminable rosary of guilts and mistakes, we offended each other, wounded each other, screamed, and waxed ironic. By dawn we didn't recognize one another. I headed for the hospital and he for the office. My stay at the doctor's provoked a paranoia about the juvenile viruses which surrounded us, ran over us, and would rejoice if they caught us unprepared. Finally there I was standing on 17th Street which is for me the most attractive and saddest street in Vedado, under a sun which was shedding its rays with a verticality completely lacking in imagination. I was tired, trying to move through a petrified city, and dividing what energy I had left between two things: carrying Victor Manuel and thinking that the sole bright spot in my life was the rigorous weight control which prevented me from being, today, a complete Neapolitan mama.

Sabina appeared so as to put some motion into a scene whose tempo was otherwise worthy of a Tarkovski film. So as to interpose herself like a knight errant between the weak and the inevitable, between my frustration and the inertia of the asphalt. So as to handle my problems the way I handle Victor's falls and his crying. Reminding me, from her dimension, of my own. And showing off her pagan trinity: ambition, pragmatism, and success.

We almost didn't talk. I, because I was controlling the excesses of Victor Manuel, and she because she supposed (surely correctly) that we no longer spoke the same language. I didn't have to ask in order to know that she had everything she wanted, and what she didn't have would soon be conquered by her energy and desire. I didn't speak much of myself, not having anything to tell her. My life doesn't meet even the minimum standards which her ears require. I think that I was grateful for her tolerant and understanding silence. When we said goodbye she kept looking at Victor, who was fighting desperately to jump from my arms and kick stones from the yard to the door. So I invited her to the birthday party and repented before I was done speaking; but afterwards I thought that she must have forgotten it immediately and, after an instant of commiserating silence, proceeded on her journey of conquest aboard a train which I could only stand and watch pass me by.

Sabina drives and thinks that the car is for shit and that all the mechanics together ought to form a guild and baptize themselves "Ali Baba's forty thieves." Whenever they fix one thing they leave something else broken, she thinks, some tiny problem which is never evident the first day but grows steadily. When she brings the car in and tells the story, this one looks at her with an expression somewhere between pity and amusement, and treats her the way pediatricians treat new mothers who trust them with their children without realizing that the doctors never really know what's wrong. Verónica's baby has a cold, but for that there's no need to go to the doctor: lots of liquid, an expectorant, and steam. But Verónica is respectful and obedient. No, it's that she's lazy, she likes to have others think for her, so she doesn't strain her brain. Verónica lets herself be led . . . and everything turns out fine. She's a young, pretty mother whom everyone helps with her strong and healthy baby. Sergio adores her, and she maintains toward everyone that languid air of someone who condescendingly allows people to love her.

Enviable ennui, without any struggle. Verónica does us the favor of letting us in, but never manages to love us because that would require strength she doesn't have, not for this purpose at least. I think she doesn't love herself much either.

She's been majestic since she was a little girl. She never made loud requests, nor even laughed stridently. She never was the center; royalty never are, instead it's the buffoons, the gladiators, the Christians, and everybody who serves them. No outlandish hairstyles or outfits, friendly and distant with everyone, not too interested in anything, not even in me.

The day I decided we were going to be friends began with a paradox. This business of imitating people is a bit like trying on clothes to see what fits us best. Of course there's always one dress which we don't even try on because we can see it's not for us. That's what happened with her. Just as a fat girl doesn't wear a tight waist, I couldn't dare to be like that pastel tone of Verónica's because to do so I would have needed her aura, and I wasn't born that way. She was a normal person, neither manic nor muddled. Nothing, no superlatives at all. She was fantastically ordinary, with every ingredient in exact proportion. Like clothes that are discreet and elegant, and we don't know what it is about them, and it's simply that they are well cut. I didn't have this spiritual peace, nor this psychic harmony. I didn't have enough faith in myself to allow myself the luxury of being simple. I wanted to sit beside her because it was impossible to sit inside her. I could incorporate anything, except her confidence in normality—I could deck myself out in anything that attracted attention, but not exhibit a simple nudity like hers.

I showed my disdain for her character because I was defending myself against an impossible desire to rest. Now I'm a mature woman and I still haven't rested, my head doesn't get *days off*. Everyone around me constitutes an arid and inhospitable land, in which I am a settler prepared to fight to establish myself in their lives, and I find it terribly exhausting. To be remembered requires a lot of calories. I can't go through life as unadorned as Verónica, because I don't have her astral protection; I don't need it, of course.

I fantasize that people's souls and destinies are recorded in the form of clinical histories or work records, stored in something like the pigeonholes behind the desk of a hotel. The guardian angels request them and study them like doctors with their patients' charts. And Verónica's angel takes care of her as if she were permanently in Intensive Care. That angel has got a lot of work, because his charge goes through life leaving him to deal with the thieves, the drunk drivers, the bad friends, the undertow at the beach, the rabid dogs, and the adulterous mate. I think this good gentleman might perhaps want to watch over me, since I'm more cooperative, but if he's seeking consecration, Verónica is a magnificent proposition for him. When all is said and done, guardian angels are merely men, and this one has to be a knight-protector in love with a damsel in distress.

Men don't like intelligent women. I can't tolerate stupid men, and therefore I haven't married and my sentimental life is reduced to going to bed with a brilliant and affected soul who philosophizes from his shoelaces to his hemoglobin during an orgasm, about, among other things, the impossibility of breaking up his family of one idiot woman and two girls. What a harem! To be truthful, I think the best thing about him is that he doesn't put me first. If one day he did, I'd run in fear from the catastrophic design called marriage, invented by men who are incapable of living without someone to represent, encourage, and help them—their wives doing all this with the "lack of pity characteristic of women," as I read in the best book of a pedantic and imaginative author. Well, men do like intelligent women such as Verónica. Such as me, no. I'm merely intelligent, neurons without hormones. Not even the guy I know who is most fanatical about female intelligence was for me.

Of course, now he's married to Verónica. I think I loved him a lot and I think too that I could have married him. I could have cooked for him and staged jealous scenes (requirements that not even Marguerite Yourcenar can fail to meet if she wants to maintain a marriage). God, he was quite a guy! He called me "the trivial Sabina." We had an unbelievable relationship, comradely, sexy, elusive. We never said we loved each other, nor that we'd get married, nor have children, nor any of those kitschy things. So now he's married to someone else and I haven't seen him since. I stored him away with a kind of mystical lust, and now, like all the important memories of our lives, he's got neither odor nor flavor nor evocative atmosphere. The dust of the divine and intangible has covered him with a curtain which we can't open again.

I gave him to Verónica. She didn't flirt with him, she behaved most properly and agreeably. One day I found a Grand Funk cassette in her house. "It's Sergio's. He likes 'Locomotion.' Not me,

I prefer 'Bad Time.' He lent me this book, too." Suddenly I understood that Sergio was an idiot and Vero another one, that they were going to have a delicious and enviable romance and that they were two compatible souls in a dimension I didn't know. Literature and music. Lending books and cassettes. A poor means for beginning an *affaire*. These artifacts have the miserly task of saying to the other person what one has neither the strength nor the talent to offer. Incredibly, they act as a Rorschach test. Somebody who reads the magazine *Hola* and listens to Juan Gabriel hasn't got anything to talk about with somebody who listens to Joaquín Sabina and likes *A Confederacy of Dunces*. Verónica and Sergio listen to Victor Manuel and read *The Tin Drum*. Their diagnoses are similar.

They have a baby. Pretty (like all of them). He seems to have been well-conceived. He looked at me and laughed. He's an atom. He touched everything in the car. The mystery of motherhood is unfathomable, a long sadomasochistic chain, one-way and irreversible. I always hear mothers telling long stories about the enormous amount of work a child requires, but evidently the balance is positive because the earth's population keeps growing despite the fact that everyone agrees the planet is becoming a terrifying place to live. But since so far it's the only one we've got . . .

Verónica must be living through sleepless nights, with all the consequences: wrinkles, grey hairs, physical and mental fatigue. She's no longer mistress of her time, and her person takes second place. Her house and life are a terrible mess, but it has to be an enchanting one, decreed by this little two-year-old who is a full-time Pandora's box.

I haven't had much to do with babies. This implies that I sleep as much as I want, my clothes aren't full of drool, and I'm not required to make telephone calls in order to change my plans. My charms are intact and I don't need anyone.

She told me she's still working in the same place. In truth Verónica is smart, logical, and intuitive, and she has the sensibility and the anguish of artists and geniuses, but only the two of us know this. In school she was like that, reached brilliant conclusions, made the abstract concrete, and had a didactic but naive way of explaining things that made you think this idea could just as well have occurred to anyone. She was never aggressive nor made herself noticed, yet all the teachers and classmates knew that she was "special."

Today she must be the same, admired from a respectful distance which she defines in some imperceptible way, working effortlessly toward magnificent results, with everyone inclined to offer her the necessary information and advice: the women platonically captivated and the men bearing the imprint of her *languid sex appeal*, Marguerite Gautier style, which traps you like a cleft in the ice.

I supposed someday we'd see each other again. Meanwhile, I didn't bring up her name with mutual friends, although I wished very much that someone would tell me about her. That's how I knew she was still married to Sergio, that they were happy, that they had a son, that Verónica always asked about me, with the tranquil curiosity which comes from knowing we are superior, and that she had the spiritual generosity to be happy for whatever good things might have happened to me. I believe the best hasn't happened to me yet. That's going to be my dying. I suppose I'm the only person who's going to die for the pleasure of it: then and there I'm going to stop fighting with myself and with others. If anything terrifies me (and I've become a rabid atheist) it's eternal life. It must be exhausting to live forever, without end. Like a train without a final station. But I'm going to rest. To sleep the way you sleep in a good hotel when, after a shower, you close the curtains and throw yourself onto a comfortable bed that's the temperature you want, without thinking about anything except how comfortable you are. I've never been like that. I've always had something making me uncomfortable, something lacking or something too much.

I'm not a Libra and I don't have the slightest sense of the equilibrium I've always sought. My scales tip, inevitably, because of details which over-color or else blanch parts of my life. My professional life is full-to-bursting, disordered and baroquely paranoid, replete with potential enemies, undesirable replacements, guileful questions, equivocal intentions, and court dialogs—in sum, this erosion of my energy which is the exorbitant price of a few crumbs of success. On the other hand, my emotional life is as empty and boring as a school hallway on an afternoon of classes. In my hallway there will never be children. I don't know whether I need them, but I do know that I'm alone and those who surround me either hate me or flatter me, but no one loves me. I'm not "loveable" like Verónica.

When I saw her I wanted to kiss her, to touch her hair, to say she looked pretty, with a son whom I could love like my own. I wanted to go and live her life with Sergio, Victor, and their guardian angels. She was standing on the sidewalk with the baby in her arms. Like a Renaissance madonna. Or one of those photos that illustrate UNICEF calendars. I stopped the car and I think it also stopped by itself, as astonished as I. I got out, opened the door, and she got in. I took her home to her house. I opened the door again, and she got out. An obedient chauffeur providing efficient service. As if I were the RCA Victor dog, and she the master's voice. There are some who are born to exercise a very sweet tyranny over those around them. Our conversation in the car was banal, yet I know she's still the same as ever. She invited me to the birthday of Victor Manuel (I only think of you . . . nobody in this

world can be so happy). Of course I won't go (I only think of you
. . . hand in hand, there in the garden they stand). It has taken me
many years to get beyond the frustration of not being her. To be,
again, so close to everything I want and don't have, would be
throwing so many years of iron spiritual discipline overboard. I
can't give myself the luxury of a relapse.

Aida Bahr, born 1958, lives in Santiago de Cuba. She is the author of two collections of stories, *There's a Cat in the Window* (1984) and *Women at Night* (1989), and several screenplays. "The Scent of Limes" is previously unpublished.

Translated by Dick Cluster

The Scent of Limes

The two men in uniform are walking down the middle of the street. The one in front is Emeterio, I don't know the other. They see me when they've already gotten to the steps, and they stop short. Emeterio stands there looking at me. The other one takes off his cap and mops his forehead with a handkerchief. It's something bad, real bad. I've felt it in the air since I got up, so much silence and now them, here.

"Is Iris home?"

I don't have to answer, because Iris comes into the kitchen and heads for the door with the same walk as always. In the doorway she shakes her head to get the hair out of her eyes, leans against the frame, and puts her hand on her hip. Iris the devil. Emeterio has to bow his head and when he raises it he doesn't say hello.

"I have to talk to you."

"Come in."

They start to, but stay piled up just inside the door.

"Tell the girl to leave."

"The girl is twelve. What's the story?"

The girl, that's me. I start to sweat and almost shiver with cold, and I swallow and swallow because I can't come up with any saliva to move this ball that's stuck in my throat. I'm nailed to the floor when I want to run for the beach. Iris wants me to hear what Emeterio came to tell her — he, who was never supposed to set foot in this house. In four years he's never even come close to the door. This is Aníbal's house.

Aníbal is the sea and a hope. He has long arms with muscles that look like chains under his skin, and thick veins about to burst. He smells of iodine, of salt, and you can smell it in every corner of this house.

"The one who built it is as crazy as you are."

That's what Iris said, laughing, the night we arrived here and saw that the front door led right to the kitchen and then the bathroom hallway and the bedroom and then at the end came the living room with a door and steps that go to the sea, to a strip of sand that can't measure more than two meters at low tide. I thought the house was backwards, but Aníbal showed me the sea through the open door and explained that real visitors would come to those steps by boat.

"And if the ocean swallows up the house?"

"That's what the stilts are for. If the sea rises this far, the house will float and we'll go sailing in it."

That's been Aníbal, ever since: something good waiting to happen, a wooden house that looks out on the sea with its back to the dust of the street. They put my bed in the living room next to the window, and the first nights the sound of the waves kept me awake, and so did the creaking of the house turned into a ship and Aníbal's murmurs and panting breath on the other side of the thin wall. I stretched out in the bed, licked the salt that splashed onto my lips, and felt that he, the house, and the sea were an enormous, excited animal that moistened and enveloped me.

Emeterio is sitting, the other policeman is still standing by the door turning his cap in his hands. They're not speaking because of Iris's eyes, black and hard as stones. The same thing happened to Grandma the day she came looking for me.

"I have to talk to you."

"Talk."

But Iris cut off the words with her eyes, so Grandma sat down and started twisting her handkerchief. Emeterio doesn't have anything in his hands, so he's pretending to look at the floorboards as if he were counting them. Really he's waiting for Iris to look the other way. Grandma found an easier way out of her fix.

"Can you give me a glass of water?"

Grandma seemed older and shorter. Through the window we'd seen her coming, bent over, listing to her left like a little boat dragging its anchor. Aníbal saw her first.

"Here comes your mother. I better leave if we're going to avoid an argument."

I wanted to go with him, but he held me down in my chair.

"Stay here. Your grandma will want to see you."

Iris opened the door and waited, but standing straight, not leaning. She doesn't greet women the same way she does men. At first it seemed like Grandma wasn't going to dare come in, and then like she wasn't going to be able to speak her piece, even if, as usual, it was a message from The Lord. But when Iris turned around to get her the water, she managed to free her tongue.

"They found Aníbal's boat out to sea."

Emeterio's voice comes out hoarse and it hangs there as if there's more to come. I feel the scream that wants to blow that ball out of my throat, but Iris looks at me and I can't scream. That's how she looked at me while she listened to Grandma's voice.

"You took him away from his family. That's a sin worse than lust. His wife says she'll kill herself if he doesn't come back. Her blood will be on your conscience, and you'll be responsible if that boy is left without a home."

By the way she's pressing her lips together it's clear that Iris is about to burst out laughing. She always laughs very loud, and I do too. I used to be ashamed of that because Grandpa said it was indecent. That's one of my memories: Iris leaning back in a chair, shaken by a laugh that brought tears to her eyes, and Grandpa thundering crazily that no daughter of his behaved like that, that he didn't want to see her laughing at the men's dirty stories any more. Grandpa's face got redder and redder as if Iris's laughter were forcing more and more blood to his head, so it would explode out of his eyes, his nose, his ears . . . I felt the blow and the laughter stopped; I didn't want to look any more, I crawled under the bed to get away from Grandpa's shouting. Years later, every time I burst out laughing, I'd seem to hear him again—"only whores laugh like that"—and I'd shut my mouth, until the day Aníbal took me to play at the beach and just as I was going to stop laughing he took me by the hands and said:

"I fell in love with Iris because she laughed like that."

"So he left."

Iris uses the same tone as she used when she answered Grandma, and she doesn't laugh this time either, even if it seems like she's going to. She looks at me the way she did then, as if I seem different or she wants to make me understand something.

"So if she wants to hang herself, let her go find a rope."

Grandma crossed herself in fear. But this time, Emeterio looks at Iris straight on.

"Did he talk about leaving the country?"

Iris goes to the table and serves two cups of coffee. They drink it as if it were good, though in fact it's cold. Emeterio, the other policeman, and Iris too look like ghosts; the air is gray and bears down on me. When Iris answers, her lips move before her voice comes out.

"He was acting strange since he got a letter from his brother a few days ago."

It's a lie, it's all lies. Aníbal can't have left. Without Aníbal this house would fall down.

"You're going to burn in the fires of hell forever."

All the sadness in the world in Grandma's voice, and all the rage in the words that Iris almost spit back at her.

"But until I die, I've got a house nobody can make me leave."

Aníbal's house is Iris's. He gave it to her as a present the night we arrived, and said that his wife had never liked it; so he built another one far from the sea, and he left this one empty knowing that some day he'd come back with the right woman to live in it. Iris hugged him and kissed him on the mouth and I went into the kitchen. Iris doesn't like me to watch her when she's with a man. I felt happy because we had a house and not that room where Emeterio had stuck us.

Every house has its smells and its sounds. Grandpa's house smelled of onions and coffee and in the morning what woke me was him coughing and clearing his throat in the next room. Grandpa was coughs, coffee, and a cigar between his teeth; Grandma, an apron and lots of prayers, on her knees before the Sacred Heart. The afternoon Grandpa kicked Iris out of the house, Grandma started spouting prayers one after another, hugging me so tight I couldn't move. I was speechless when a suitcase came flying out of the bedroom door and landed in the parlor, in front of Iris, and Grandpa announced the sentence at the top of his lungs:

"I don't want you under my roof another day."

Iris stuck out her chin, challenging him.

"As long as I went out with whites you didn't care, but because this one is black . . ."

Grandma let go of me and ran to get between them. Grandpa left, shouting that he didn't want to see the slightest trace of Iris when he got back.

"Give me the child. She's innocent."

The voice echoes in the kitchen as if it were that day. I was scared then. Where she should have come for me was in Emeterio's room, always full of the smell of dust and humidity, of the quarrels and cries of the neighbor women . . .

"Your mother is the mistress of a Negro. She thinks she's somebody because she's a policeman's mistress."

I would have been happy to go back then, even if I'd had to go to her church every Sunday. I liked the temple because of the singing, but I was afraid of it too, because Grandma seemed like another person, groaning and even getting terrible shakes sometimes. But Grandma never came to Emeterio's room. And now he's here, after four years in which I only bumped into him on the street, on the way to or from school. One day he stood there looking at me and I said hi.

"How's your mom?"

"Iris is fine."

Of course we were fine, the two of us, with Aníbal, in his wooden houseboat, where it smelled like salt, iodine, and limes.

Iris tosses an envelope on the table. The stamps have been cut off with scissors, and when Emeterio opens it you can see it's empty.

"Where's the letter?"

"I don't know. He didn't show it to me."

If I could only cry . . . My face is burning and I don't know if it's from the effort of holding in the tears or from Iris's eyes on me like glowing coals.

"Give me the child. She's innocent."

If only Emeterio would say something so that Iris would have to turn away. I can't stand any more. I want to run into the sea and shout Aníbal's name.

"What time did he leave the house?"

"At eight, after supper. He didn't sleep here."

Iris has said this very seriously, with a soft voice that sounds like Grandma's, but this doesn't surprise Emeterio, he doesn't notice anything, not even how long Iris has been staring at me.

Everything seems fine to him, because he leans back in the chair and his face relaxes. He tells the other policeman to go to the dock and ask if anyone saw Aníbal take his boat out last night. And Grandma leans over the table like that other time.

"Don't think of having a child by him. God keep you from that."

Aníbal wanted to have more children. Iris never wanted any. I know. In Emeterio's house and here too I've always slept very close to her bed. While she's got a man on top of her, Iris doesn't talk; you can't even hear her breathe. But she likes to talk when they're lying next to each other and she thinks I'm asleep. That's how I know. That way, and because Grandma showed me the wedding pictures.

"Look, that's your father there."

Only I forget what he looked like, because Iris didn't bring the album when we left the house. All of I've got is the idea of a skinny boy with a frightened expression. Iris, though, looked like a woman even though she was fifteen. I'm in the photo too, although Grandma never told me that. I know that I'm there, in Iris's belly, making her say yes and sign. When she gave birth she went three days without touching me, without even looking at me. On the third day she got up and put me to her breast because she thought she'd go crazy listening to me cry all the time. I know, although nobody has told me, that Iris hoped I'd die during those days. She hated me and hated Grandpa for forcing her to marry and have the baby. What I never really understood is why she took me when she left the house.

"Give me the child. She's innocent."

Emeterio livens up when the other policeman leaves. His voice sounds different.

"Were you two having problems?"

Iris smiles mockingly like that other time, tough again.

"Don't you always say it's up to The Lord whether a child should be born or not?

"That man only has abnormal ones."

Aníbal said it was his wife's fault. He told me one day at the beach. That's why he didn't want to have any more children; but with Iris he did want to.

"If she could have you, so pretty, when she was just fifteen, think what she could give me now."

That was a long time ago, when Aníbal was only the sea. For months he talked about the children he wanted. Then he didn't talk about it any more. Iris told him that she couldn't, that she'd been sterilized years before. I don't know whether this was true. Iris knows how to lie so that nobody can tell. She might have been lying when she told Emeterio:

"It wasn't me he was dissatisfied with."

The sun is shining on my back, casting my shadow on the table like a stain that covers the coffee cups.

"Do you think he's going to send for you?"

Suddenly I can breathe and the knot in my throat dissolves. I realize my bladder is bursting and I press my knees together for fear I'm going to pee here standing up.

"My daughter stays with me."

"What will become of her when she grows up?"

All the sadness in the world in Grandma's voice.

"And wasn't it you who brought me up?

That's not what Iris says. I don't hear it but it doesn't matter, because Emeterio smiles and his teeth shine very white. I run to the bathroom and slam the door. The pee gushes out without stopping while I look at Aníbal's shirt hanging from the nail and his boots, like always, on the crossbeam.

Aníbal went around the house in his undershirt. When he came in he'd take off his shirt and hang it up, and then he'd drop into one of the chairs. The dark hair of his chest showed, and the veins of his neck stuck out almost as much as those of his arms. I washed his shirts and undershirts, and I'd smell them before putting them in the water. I liked to watch how he took them off, how the cloth would rise up and his broad back would appear, burned by the sun and the salt. Once I put on one of those undershirts. I looked at myself in the mirror over the dresser. On me it was enormous. In the front you could see as far as the mole I have in the middle of my chest, right between my breasts that were just beginning to show below the cloth. I looked myself over in the mirror and thought that Aníbal was right: I was going to be as pretty as Iris. Then I heard the kitchen door open.

"Give me the child. She's innocent."

Iris is still sitting facing Emeterio. The sun is shining on the table but the cups aren't there any more.

"I'll let you know if we find out anything."

"It's nothing to me."

Iris looks at me again, and now she's calm.

"Anyone who leaves me, I forget him right away. This one's father, I don't even remember his name."

Emeterio gets to his feet. He's very tall. The things about him that caught my attention, when I started living in that room, were the yellow of his eyes, his little ears, and his big, flat nose. His face was all I noticed. I didn't care about his body at all.

"If I can help you with anything, let me know."

And it's Grandma who's at the door, her foot reaching for the top stair.

"If you change your mind, let me know."

The door closes behind his uniform. The kitchen looks big and abandoned.

Iris stands up, puts the chairs back in their places and the cups in the sink. She doesn't look at me, she's got her shoulders hunched and her mouth ready to answer, but I don't dare ask.

"My daughter stays with me."

I run through the house and plunge into the sea, and now no one will wonder when they see my eyes. I try to swim but don't get anywhere, and then I realize I've got my clothes on. Out of the water, I slump down under the steps in the heavy gray sand covered with seaweed. My secret place.

In the house, deep silence, Iris sleeping the way she always does, on her stomach, her hair in her face, her right arm over the pillow she's put there in Aníbal's place. How many times did I see her sleeping like that, with her arm flung over his back? Someday I would do it too. It's eleven in the morning but Iris is sleeping as if it were midnight, so she's not going to know I'm opening the cabinet to look at Aníbal's clothes, the shirts I won't have to wash any more, the shoes lined up underneath. It's all here, he didn't take a thing. When we left Emeterio's room, Iris arranged every-

thing on the bed, all the clothes, the jewelry, everything Emeterio
had given her.

"Why are you leaving them?"

"It's not right for me to wear what he gave me with another
man."

Aníbal gave us this house. No other man can ever come in here.
In the bathroom I strip off my wet clothes, take Aníbal's towel,
and very slowly dry myself. I climb up on the bench and lean way
out of the window to hang the clothes on the line, but first I have
to take down Iris's black bathing suit that's waving in the wind.
When I leave the bathroom, the prints of my wet feet on the
wooden floor have already dried.

The Lord has always been with Grandma. Except when she had
Iris. Maybe it was a sin, giving her that name she took from a soap
opera. Iris never liked to pray, in the temple she'd stick out her
tongue at the pastor instead. When she was ten they caught her
with a boyfriend at school. Iris, the devil. She's got a scar on her
knee and another on her head from running around with a gang
of boys. She's been the woman of many men: she was with Emeterio for almost three years, with Aníbal for more than four.
Those are the ones that have lasted longest. When she has a man
on top of her, she doesn't speak.

"I don't give myself. I accept the man I like. It's different."

At first I didn't care how it was. Later, I wanted to take after
her.

"Like your mother, there aren't many women like her."

But something's wrong with her. No man lasts. Not even a
good one, like Aníbal. That was the first thing Grandma said the
day she came after me.

"When they told me, I couldn't believe it. They told me you were living here and I didn't believe that either. He's not for you. He's a man who looks after his home and his son."

Aníbal discovered my hideout because he saw a shape under the steps.

"I thought it was a dog."

He knelt down alongside me and showed me the bag of limes. They were big and light green and gave off an aroma so strong they hid the smell of the sea. Aníbal asked whether Iris was home. Then he held one of the limes under my nose.

"Do you like it?"

He slid it softly over my lips, over my chin. He brought it down my neck and rested it at the edge of my bathing suit, between my breasts.

"I like your little limes. They're so lovely. It's okay if I touch them?"

His hands were hardened and hot. He just touched my breasts, he didn't squeeze them. I felt distressed, a great distress, a desire that this had never happened or that it would never stop. The floor creaked above us, he took his hands off without hurrying. I closed my eyes and when I opened them I was alone, surrounded by the scent of lime.

Iris looks at me over the plate. I'm furious at being hungry. I shouldn't eat anything more until he comes back. Because he's coming back.

"Cut out the foolishness and eat."

I do what she says. I always have. Iris has got this power over me, she controls me without blows or punishments because she can read my thoughts. Not only mine. My grandparents' and Emeterio's too.

"It's the devil at work."

Grandma's voice comes from far away, full of fear.

"She doesn't want me to baptize you."

I told Aníbal that I wouldn't be able to go to heaven when I died because I wasn't baptized. He carried me to the sea and threw water on my forehead. Then, back in the house, he stood me in front of the mirror so I could see there wasn't any mark on me.

"God must have a better way to tell the good from the bad."

That was at first, when Aníbal was only the sea.

It's a big cardboard box that takes up the whole center of the bed. Iris folds the clothes very carefully before putting them away. I'm horrified to see her do this. Iris covers the clothes with the hammock that Aníbal took his naps in, and she puts his shoes on top.

"They're for that woman. So she can sell them and use the money for her son."

If I could, I'd scream that this couldn't be, that when Aníbal comes back everything has to be there waiting for him.

"Forget about Aníbal."

If I close my eyes she can't keep on reading my thoughts. This isn't Aníbal's house anymore. The sea won't ever carry it off because Iris will find a way to fasten it to the earth. She'll give orders to the sea, the way she orders me to bring her the boots from the bathroom. She puts them together with the rest of the things. It's something like a burial, this putting absolutely all of a man's things into a box. When I ask, I'm more surprised by the fright in Iris's eyes than by the fact that I'm thinking out loud:

"Why did Aníbal leave barefoot?"

The tide is high and the waves are nearly licking the first step. The foam is shining in the darkness, but it doesn't make me want to look. Iris came back without the box and with a tired look that's more like sadness than any I've ever seen on her. I didn't help, I didn't even clear the plates from the table. After all, nothing worse can happen now.

She's standing behind me and she too may be looking at the sea. Iris has never done this. When she and Aníbal went down to the beach at night they went to walk, to swim. They never sat on the steps. He only did that with me. If she's come now it's to tell me something. She doesn't speak because she's looking for the way to say it. If I looked, I'd see the same expression on her face as when she used to try to remember the fairy tales that I asked her to tell me. She was very good at telling stories, because she livened them up with different voices and even acted them out. Those were the only happy times in Emeterio's room. Before, in Grandpa's house, Iris didn't tell me stories. Every night, Grandma took it on herself to tell me stories about Jesus. I can still clearly remember the weddings of Canaan, the resurrection of Lazarus. But I liked the fairy tales better, fairies and princes and mice drowned in pots . . .

"I always dreamed of going to Havana. Of dancing and singing in a cabaret. I saw myself dressed in a little outfit of lamé and sequins

and a long feather train. Every time they caught me rumba dancing, Mama set me to praying instead."

Iris's voice sounds different, quieter and kind of sad. I want to
look at her, but I resist because it would nearly amount to a pardon and I don't want to do that.

"I wish I could still dream."

She goes down the steps to the sand. She crouches and picks up
some seaweed. Without turning to look at me, she starts to pop
the bubbles with her fingernails. I know that now I could cry, that
Iris not only would let me but might even be grateful if I did. But
my eyes are dry. I prepare my answer, because I'm finally going to
say it.

"I thought he loved me, that he was the man I'd been looking
for."

I stand up and shout, shout so that the ocean and everyone can
hear me.

"Aníbal was strong and he was good. He was wonderful."

Iris smiles and throws the seaweed into the ocean. She comes
up slowly until she's face to face with me.

"We saw him like that. Really he was just like any other guy."

A cold wind shakes me all of a sudden. Something breaks inside
me and it hurts, hurts so much I have to cry, bent over and
trembling. Iris hugs me and I let her do it. I can't get control of this
body that jumps and shakes as if it weren't my own. I manage to
repeat between sobs that Aníbal was good.

"Sure, he was. It's just that he wanted a daughter and you
weren't his daughter. You needed a father and he was only a
man."

The weeping and trembling are letting up. It's strange how
much Iris resembles Grandma, now that her eyes look sweet and
calm. She lets me loose and I step back and bump into the railing.
Iris goes back to being the same as always.

"The important thing is that you and I are together."

She goes into the house and the boards creak, obedient to her step. The house belongs to Iris. So do I. The spray splashes the first step, and there's something humble and pleading in this wave that doesn't dare bang against the wood. The sea was the loser, and Aníbal with it. That empty boat drifting is the image of defeat, of abandonment.

I lean my head on the doorframe and close my eyes. All through the house there is the scent of limes.

Esther Díaz Llanillo, born 1934, works in the central library of the University of Havana. She received her doctorate in philosophy and literature from that university in 1959 and published stories in several Cuban anthologies of the 1960s. Her collection of stories, *The Penalty*, was published in 1966. "My Aunt" is from a new book currently in preparation.

Translated by Cindy Schuster

My Aunt

My aunt was very old. When you looked at her profile, with her slightly aquiline nose, somnolent eyes, protruding lower lip, pointed chin, and scrawny body, her appearance vaguely brought to mind those witches from the Middle Ages who used to frequent the gloomy forests of legend. But, seen from the front, my aunt was simply a helpless angel, her beautiful wings split under the profusion of an immaculate tangle of gray hair. Both visions: the terrifying and the beatific, were my aunt.

Sitting in her sick woman's armchair, moving unsteadily on

someone's arm, begging, asking for things, demanding, expecting us to wait on her hand and foot: without us my aunt did not exist and with her, we could not exist.

Her quick puppeteer's hands manipulated us like fragile marionettes, bouncing us from one end of her stage to the other. It was the venerable and venerated right of her fervent old age. Her daily and nightly rituals transformed us into nothing more than acolytes whose only right was to wait.

But to wait, for what? Her voice, her command, her plea, her cry, her panic at night when it seems the moment of her death has arrived, her sleeping among the shadows: bony face pale and serene; fingers pressed together as if in prayer; mouth half-open; her snore rattling (was she still alive?) from her deathbed.

Yet, she appears to me by day; I feel her moving nimbly behind me. I get jittery when I see her in the kitchen—her listless eyes try to say something and her mere presence is a cry of fear in the middle of the afternoon. But it's not true, my aunt is in the living room, I see her sitting in her chair surrounded by big pillows. Then I wonder: which is the face that watches me, which of my aunt's two faces?

My aunt has died. We bury her. We cry over her memory, because along with our liberation comes my aunt's absence. The house is full of that absence of her things, of her body that still seems to inhabit its familiar corners. We hide her clothes, move her furniture around. Our relief is still unable to acknowledge that pious absence which leaves us with nowhere to go, disoriented. Are we alive?

But we're not alone. Then I sense it: there, behind me, in the kitchen, she looks at me. Her body drifts towards me, it merges with mine. Her quick hands are visible in my own.

Her sterile flesh filters through my flesh. I can already feel the weight of her eyes in mine. Her toothless mouth is in my firm one. Then I understand: from this moment on and even more with every passing day, as the years go by, I am, I will be, my aunt.

Ana Luz García Calzada was born in 1944 in Guantánamo, studied Spanish language and literature at the University of Havana, and lives in Guantánamo today. She is the
author of several story collections published in Cuba, most
recently *Heavy Rock* (1995), from which "Disremembering
a Smell" is taken.

Translated by Dick Cluster

Disremembering
a Smell

The wild thing has been roaring all along the road. Every step we
take, the roar is right there with us, charging through the open
fields, disturbing the landscape of guinea grass where the cows
graze, dozens of cagaleche birds perched upon their backs. At my
side, Papa coughs and complains, and in his eyes I find a brilliance
I've never seen there before. He's looking at everything with a
meekness that astonishes me, and he's very calm and doesn't seem
to care much about the roaring and the pounding of hoofs on the
grass; I turn nervously and signal him, but he doesn't listen to me.
Papa is a very determined man and I've followed him since I was

little, both before and after Mama died. From that moment on, all this began cooking in the big cauldron of his head. I didn't really understand it, I still don't understand his desire to leave everything behind and go live over there.* Papa has these ideas way deep inside him, what he calls his skyscraper thoughts. I've never known where he got it all, he's always been this way, and he taught me this taste for the unknown, this leaning toward danger and adventure. Since we've got a hunting license, all we had to do was clean the shotguns well, put on comfortable clothes, and fill the canteens. Plus, I was attracted by that roar which only we heard, because I had a feeling that he had heard it and he guessed the same about me, though we never said a thing. We've always—or almost always—understood each other that way. Myself, I've always really enjoyed this business of hiking and proving that I can wear the pants, because you've got to wear the pants, he told me, a man has to be like that, and from the beginning. Fear and shitting your pants are for women and queers: a real man knows how to wear the pants, and do it well. That's why I followed him and I follow him, because he's my father and I'm a man and I know all about wearing the pants. The ground is shaking like it's trying to tell me something. We stop to take a rest. Papa stays still for a good while, with that lamb's face I'll never forget. There's a slight movement in the grass, but I can't make anything out. I rub my eyes but I only see the same row of tamarind trees and that huge rock on one side of the road.

A cagaleche flutters nearby, opens and closes its beak which is sure to be full of ticks, and then spreads its wings to fly higher in a smooth, almost sexy glide. The moon is a shining sickle that

* The implication is "in the U.S."

breaks the roaring of the beast in Papa's eyes. He looks at me and says that he started to notice it a long time ago, when mama got sick and the aunts filled the house with shadows and silence and doctors, and I had to go do my homework at a neighbor's house. I say, yes, me too, since that time. Then he talks to me about cheeses and metals and a penetrating odor that he had smelled since we left, until he lost it in the bed of the last truck where the force of the wind must have dispersed it, and when the truck dropped us off alongside the highway, by a solitary house that we pointed out to the driver in order to confuse him, he started to sense it again. The light was dazzling in the tumbledown stone corridor which we passed through like shadows. There were two heads in the window, one a woman's and one a man's, the two of them sitting on a couple of benches, eating, and that was when Papa heard another roar and I answered with a nod and then, for the first time, there was the smell for me. I came close to Papa's ear, cautiously, and asked him, but he didn't answer. I kept thinking about that scent, where it came from, a smell I'd never known before, that wasn't in my memory, because I've got a whole filing cabinet in my nose. They say it comes from Mama who felt the smell of death before she died, even the shades of smell in every part of her body, and they say she was horrified because she had this uncontrollable fear of worms, a terror that I inherited along with this insolent nose. You only have to tell me that there's something coming close to me, and I close my eyes, take a breath, and I'm able to identify it a good ways off, but that's not all, I can classify it too. In school nobody believed me until I showed them by hiding my eyes with a handkerchief while girls and boys filed by in front of me and I said all their names. There was a big fuss and two of them even got into a fight, one saying it was true and the other that I was a liar and we must have fixed it somehow. The biology teacher had to intervene, he looked at me with an expression that said I wasn't doing him any favors, and he said something about telepathy and I don't know what else that nobody understood, and when he left they were worse than before, and I told them the story of Mama and the worms but without admitting that I'm afraid too, because I know they could make me pay for it. I didn't tell them about the roaring, either, because then they'd say it was the same as with my nose, that I can hear from a great distance and it must be one of the animals in the zoo which is about ten blocks away. So I kept quiet and I keep quiet, because they are never going to see the carpet of fruits that cluster together under the tamarinds, nor the enormous rock, nor Papa's meek eyes. He asks if we can walk a while more, because he's afraid the dawn will surprise us in this zone riddled with sentry posts.* Papa looks at the sky to orient himself and breathes deeply, very deeply; then he signals to me and together we go on tracking the smell. And I feel like Soarez, the son of Yañez, Sandokan's friend, or I'm transfigured into Kammamuri and I want to defeat the panther of the Vindhyas.†

Papa leaves me behind and marches ahead like a hunting dog following the scent. We enter a grove of casuarina trees and hear the creaking of branches and leaves, while the cold wet breath of the ground rises around us. Above, through the canopy, we see the first rays of the sun. Papa stops walking and says we have to go back because we're lost and we'll have to put it off for another

---

* The implication is that these are Cuban sentry posts in the zone surrounding the naval base occupied by U.S. forces on Guantanamo Bay.

† Characters in the adventure novels of Emilio Salgari (1863–1911), long popular in Latin America.

time. The roar is nowhere to be heard, and the smell is behind us and sometimes gets farther away. We're going back slowly, guided by its traces. Papa and I are walking almost together, we know time is passing by the light which outlines more and more precisely the recesses of the woods. Further on we realize that we're not returning the same way we came, that now the trees are not pines but cypresses, rising up like green ribbons of flame. We turn into a very narrow passage, always with the smell guiding us like a ship's pilot. I don't ask Papa about the future, I know it well and know that we'll come back here, and he doesn't say anything either but from the way he looks at me I know it's going to be soon, because now he's not so worried about my pants, he knows I've got my long pants and I'm wearing them well. I feel like Sandokan, the Malaysian tiger, and I feel confident now.

We stop to unsling the shotguns and drink a little water. Papa watches how I caress the barrel of my Remington and point it over my nose toward a treetop. He stops me with a brusque motion and asks me if I'm crazy. He throws a stone and we hear the flapping wings of a flock of yaguazas. I lower the barrel and take another drink from the canteen. Papa's eyes grow meek again. We go into another passage, even narrower because the cypresses grow close together, and the smell is getting more intense. A swarm of wasps swipes by us and we stay very still until we see them disappear into the trees. There's a white stain far off in the next corridor of cypresses, like a padded carpet inviting us to rest. We pick up our pace and when we're almost there I let out a shriek which Papa almost makes me swallow on the spot. The ground in this place is covered with maggots which move and then stay still and seem to be talking among themselves, all of them so close together and so tangled up that I have to throw up, there against the cypress where the passageway starts. And Mama, poor Mama who was so afraid of them and who had to bear them for who knows how long. Papa makes me walk on top of them, and one retching follows another and I think I'm going to die. I think maybe that's what the smell is, and Papa and I are going to have to stay here in this place. But the passage is coming to an end and I can't help breaking into a mad dash over branches and dry leaves and worms. Papa chides me but I don't want to stop, I want to be close to the light, to feel the heat of the sun and get away as fast as I can, far away from the white worms, from the so-white worms of the milk and the cheese and the metal and the smell, so strong again, even stronger than the desire to retch and to run.

Papa comes along behind, scolding me in a low voice and shaking off the remains of the maggots that stuck to his boots. I look at mine and the vomit rises again and comes out without my being able to stop it. Papa tells me to shake off them off, but I can't, if I look at them I'll die, if I feel them I'll die, I'll die if I breathe any deeper the smell that I'm sure comes from them. Then Papa throws me on the grass and loosens my laces and pulls off my boots and carries them away to shake them where I can't see. He's doing that and he looks at me and he bangs the boots against the roots of an old ceiba and that's when we hear the roar. Papa finishes with the worms and angrily throws the boots at me. He waits impatiently and points toward the north; I follow him, a little nauseous but glad to be going back and soon I realize that we're once more facing the row of tamarinds and we're on one side of the big rock. Papa tells me to rest a while, that I'm very pale and we've still got a ways to go to get to the highway. I sit on the carpet of tamarinds, pick up one of them, peel off the rind and put a piece of the acid pulp into my mouth. This helps me get rid of the sticky awful taste left by the vomit. Papa studies the landscape, picks up a few branches, looks fearfully at a gray cloud that has come to rest in front of the sun, and stretches out his hand to see whether it's raining, but no, the atmosphere is heavy and we feel a kind of dampness that isn't ready to be rain. Papa takes a few steps toward the giant rock, looks at me from where he is, and I see once more that strange meekness in his eyes; he raises a hand and says something that I can't make out from here. I see him disappear behind the rock and I stay where I am. Suddenly, an enormous roar envelops everything and then silence and the slamming of a door. I know that it comes from there, I'm sure, and I run to see what has happened to him, but all I find is white silence, as white as the worms, the thousands of worms that are there moving on the surface of the rock.

Magaly Sánchez, born 1940, is a journalist who lives in Havana. Her novella *Fabia Tabares as Seen in the Mirror* was published in Havana in 1996, and her biography of Commander Piti Fajardo, written for children, appeared in 1980. "Catalina in the Afternoons" is previously unpublished.

Translated by Cindy Schuster

Catalina in the Afternoons

Catalina opened her eyes and felt her body drenched in sweat. She must have fallen asleep for a few minutes and once again she found herself in the suffocating afternoon heat. She looked outside. The fierce midday light fell upon the nearby remains of a deteriorated structure, eaten away by rainstorms, scorched by the suns of innumerable days. She noticed that two more flowers had blossomed on the vine that was turning green upon the ruins. She knew everything that happened on those fragments of stones and dusty mortar thanks to a mute dialogue she held hour after hour, day after day, by that passing of her glance over the surface stained by dampness, eroded by time. And Good Lord, how boring it was to look and look at the battered mass. But the doctor had ordered her to rest, to remain practically immobile, until the bone of her leg knit together. "We will not permit such a lovely extremity to lose its shape, Señora," he had said gallantly. More than a week had passed since then and she'd grown weary of plucking the strings of her mandolin, of having the servants tell her stories, of tempting her palate with sweet and tart delicacies and flavors invented just for her. Now her body asked only to ride horseback through the outskirts of the city in the fresh air and sun, to run back and forth through the rooms of the house, and to stop by the kitchen to gossip with the servant girls. Above all, she felt the desire to fulfill her young body's demands for pleasure, a feeling which grew increasingly imperative during the midday torpor and the stifling nights.

It had been several months since her husband, Don Diego, had set sail on the long crossing to the Metropolis. Starved for affection, she had taken refuge in the caresses of the handsome gardener from the neighboring manor. Her relationship with the servant had shown her that there were others more accomplished than her husband in the art of love, and that the depth of her pleasure was a bottomless well. Only recently had her body allowed its deepest resonances to be heard, and her uninhibited cries of pleasure had pierced the thin walls of the hut where the gardener kept his tools—just a few yards from the dividing wall that separated the gardens of the two houses. It was a love nest cradled by the suffocating heat of the night, refreshed every now and then by sea breezes seasoned with the smells of salt and iodine, and perfumed with honeysuckle and jasmine; a fragrance tinged with the vapor of organic matter fermenting on an earth dampened by daily cloudbursts. It was during her last night with Cándido that the accident occurred. After that night's hours of love, at the distant call of the watchman announcing the stroke of four o'clock, the lovers headed for the wall she was obliged to scale, as on previous nights, so that she might return home before the servants began their bustling about. The moment having arrived, he positioned himself next to the wall and bent over, offering her his back as a stair. She stepped on it with somewhat more force than was desirable with the thick heels of her wet, muddy boots, grasped the highest part of the wall firmly with her hands, and hoisted herself over. But she pushed too hard and, finding no support, fell to the other side, where she lay sprawled on the ground, biting her hands to keep from howling with pain.

"What happened, my love?" asked Cándido, in a voice both solicitous and hushed.

"Oh, I've had an accident!" she answered between whimpers.

Immediately, his head appeared above the wall.

"I'll go with you, darling, I'll help you."

"May God prevent you!" she hurriedly responded. "I will get to my room as best I can. Leave, quickly, don't let anyone find us."

He instantly complied with her wish and Catalina sat up with difficulty. One of her legs hurt so badly that it could barely support her and so, limping, clinging to the trunk of one small tree after another, leaving shreds of her dress in their branches, she reached the rear of the house and finally her bedroom. She hardly knew how she managed it, but the fact is that when Doña Acacia, a kind of servant and personal attendant of hers, brought her breakfast in bed, as was customary, she found Catalina in a cheerful mood, her face bearing no visible traces of the dreadful night she had passed. With a voracious appetite and the most refined manners, Catalina polished off two roast partridges, a large round loaf of bread, and a bowl of café au lait. At the end of the meal she licked her lips; though it is impossible to say whether this signified her satisfaction with the tasty delicacies or with her memories of the previous night.

"You slept well, Señora. I can tell from looking at your face." Doña Acacia said this as she finished removing the mosquito netting that covered the bed, so that the sun and the morning air might circulate freely. "Now, you must rise; you said you wanted to go to mass."

"Yes, of course," answered Catalina, and not remembering her injury, as the soreness had subsided during the immobility of sleep, she made an attempt to move her legs out of the bed, but felt a stab of pain in the injured limb. She cried out, with such force that every last hair of Doña Acacia's abundant mane stood on end.

"Holy Mary! What is it, Señora? Speak!"

"Oh, Acacia," sobbed Catalina. "I had already forgotten about it. Last night, half-asleep, I ran into an armchair on my way to the bathroom, and the pain was so terrible that I could barely make it back to my bed, where I fainted into sleep, until just now when I awoke."

"Let me see, Señora," and the servant carefully took her leg. "My Lord!" she exclaimed as soon as she saw the injury, "It's as swollen as a ham! I'll send for the doctor."

"Do it, Acacia dear," she moaned, terrified at the sight of her leg so thick and discolored.

So it was that Catalina found herself confined to bed for quite some time. To distract herself, apart from looking at the ruins, she would imagine the activity around the port a hundred yards away, which came to life soon after daybreak, with the entry of some ship sporting a boisterous crew and brightly colored rigging. At night, when the darkness of the streets discouraged the occasional transit of noisy carriages, the festive music of the slums began to take over the nocturnal silence: a music which spread through the air entangled with the secret language and peals of laughter of sailors and whores. But in the steamy afternoons, time would grow hushed, hypnotic, and she would have only enough energy to cast her gaze upon the weather-beaten structure within her view. During one of those afternoons, as she looked without seeing—from having looked so much at the dusty façade and the latest blossoms on the vine—something new caught her eye: a black dove, with a broad and iridescent breast, had perched there, on a projection of the jagged cornice. The little animal was walking around in small circles, pecking between his feet. "He's snacking on ants," Catalina said to herself and then realized that she was too far away to see any ants. "Ha, how foolish of me, how could I possibly see them from here?" And she began to wonder if they were black or red and whether or not they bit. "Eat them up, dear, especially if they're tiny and red, because they are demons. Yesterday they ruined my hands, just because there were crumbs on them from the sweet bread I had for tea."

The dove quieted down at last, settling his broad, plumed breast upon his legs, which disappeared among his feathers.

Catalina's interest in the crumbling edifice grew after that. Every afternoon, at almost exactly the same time, after the daily cloudbursts had thrashed the city to a quagmire and while the sun began to dry the wet surfaces, the dove would parade before her eyes. She enjoyed the beauty and activity of the bird. "I wonder whose dovecote he escaped from?" she asked herself on more than one occasion. When the dove took flight and left, she would feel that time was once again a petrified thing and her attention would return to more mundane concerns. She would listen to the gossip of the maidservants rising from the ground floor. Real chatterboxes, they were in the habit of commenting on the day's events as they rested by the cool of the fountain in the shade of a dense vine, when the morning's work was done. Then she would feel that the heat was driving her mad and the torpor of the afternoon, combined with the gurgling of the waters flowing endlessly from the fountain, would make her eyelids heavy. And thinking about how she would arrange a rendezvous with Cándido, she would fall asleep.

"Good Heavens, how hot it is!" It was Doña Acacia, who awakened her with great commotion. She was talking animatedly and carrying a piping hot bowl of broth. She put the candlestick with its burning candle on the table.

"Drink your broth, Señora. Whet your appetite because I ordered them to prepare some garbanzo beans that, God knows, make my mouth water."

Catalina brought the bowl to her mouth and was captivated by the aroma of chicken stock with garlic and onion. She savored the broth, detecting, as well, that subtle touch of a few leaves of cilantro, wisely added at the last moment, so that their flavor wouldn't overpower that of the other spices.

"Ah, this restores my appetite!" she said with a sigh when she finished drinking the broth.

"Good Lord!" exclaimed the servant, crossing herself, "I didn't know you had lost it, Señora."

Catalina was not in the habit of conversing much with Doña Acacia, but ever since she found herself confined to bed, this had become another distraction from the long hours of boredom. In comparison with Catalina's extreme youth, Doña Acacia, an unrefined woman in her forties, seemed ancient. Moreover, she was Don Diego's confidant, and Catalina had always been careful to keep her in the dark about her escapades. These were mere frivolities that barely qualified as mischief, like riding horseback in the rain or going for a swim, alone and naked, in some nearby pool. Whims that would have left her husband beside himself, had he known about them, for which reason she was accustomed to committing these small sins in secret. However, that other matter, getting involved with another man, was something new. They had married her off when her breasts had barely sprouted and she had taken a fancy to her husband because he was young and strong; but he had been away for a long time and his absence aroused her most ardent desires. Her longing for Cándido's lovemaking, and her inability to meet him again, filled her with desperation. Confined to her bed, she could hardly expect to communicate with the gardener because he would never dare to visit her (under what pretext?). And it was even less likely that Cándido would avail himself of an intermediary to send her even a few words of comfort. And not because he was a gentleman, which he wasn't, but because everyone for miles around knew about Don Diego's bad temper; he was a renowned hothead. Catalina was going on like this, racking her brains to find a way to alleviate her situation, when Doña Acacia returned carrying a brilliantly white platter in which a generous portion of roast pork proclaimed its delights. She was followed by two servants bearing additional platters, including the previously announced garbanzo dish, rice, and stewed vegetables, as well as a pitcher of water and a bottle of red wine. Catalina knew that after she ate, her stuffed belly and the heat would make her suffer for a couple of hours, but she was never able to control herself. That's how it went, from the pleasures of a good meal to the tortures of hell, but she eventually recovered and got in the mood to play cards with the servants for a while. Finally she fell asleep as if she'd been struck on the head. At dawn the din of the birds in the trees of the garden woke her. She heard the horses neighing as they were taken out of the stables. She caught whiffs of her delicious breakfast invading the rooms with the provocative aroma of coffee and boiled milk. She idled a good while between the sheets until she decided to do her daily toilette, assisted by Doña Acacia. This done, she put on a fine linen dressing gown, full of ribbons and smocking, breakfasted succulently, and prepared to endure one more day of desperation. After employing dozens of ruses to amuse herself through the morning, it was time for lunch and then siesta. She awoke immersed in the stifling afternoon and from that moment resorted to all the tricks she could think of to fill the disquieting emptiness of the next few hours, such as embroidering and sewing, combing and recombing her hair, eating voraciously and playing cards with the servants; but still she drifted through that time of abandonment with the certainty of bodily misery. At this point she would even have been happy for the return of the ships and with them Don Diego. She didn't even dream about an encounter with Cándido because that would have been asking for too much. When she finished ruminating she once again rested her gaze on the neighboring ruins. She looked at the ash-gray mass saturated with light, the cracks in the walls, the greenness of the vine somewhat withered by the afternoon heat and a blackish-green patina, produced by the dampness, that covered everything. She remained like this for long minutes, until she began to feel a vague sensation of restlessness. She wondered what was disturbing her.

A few seconds later she heard strong wing beats and the dove with the iridescent feathers came into view. A little light of excitement erased the tedium from her eyes. There was the bird, her dove (because she now considered him to be "her dove"). He was beautiful: his broad, throbbing, crop bursting with life, and his gracefully moving head, pecking voraciously between the cracks in the walls, so far-removed from flight that he seemed to belong to the piece of wall where he was perched. She felt he was all hers; she savored him like a novelty that spiced up the dull afternoon with a mysterious itch. She caressed him with her gaze and her mind began to play with the bird's image. Didn't he resemble an armored knight in a dark cape? That was it! A knight transformed into a bird, by some sorcerer's arts. "You are beautiful, my knight, do you know that?" she murmured, and she believed that the dove heard her in the distance and that he also regarded her attentively. And she unbraided her hair for him, so that he might admire how all that fairness fell upon her shoulders. She imagined that the bird understood that this offering of beauty was meant for him and that that was why he stood still, his upright head tilting rhythmically from side to side in order to observe her, first with one eye, then the other. Until the bird felt the call of space and took to the air with his noble face, his cape, and his sword.

From that moment on Catalina no longer experienced the afternoons as a thick and exasperating substance; they became instead a condition of desire, of being and not being in herself that culminated in a singular ecstasy. She waited for each new encounter with the bird attired in her most beautiful dressing gowns, with her hair brushed and gleaming, smelling like chamomile and falling upon her shoulders, and adorned with a red flower like a bright and throbbing clot of blood behind her ear. Under the pretext of wishing to sleep in complete tranquillity, she had forbidden anyone to disturb her during these afternoons. And had it not been for the vital necessity of eating and the obligatory assistance in doing her toilette, she would have shut herself up in her room forever, so as not to see anybody. But this being impossible, she was delighted with the long summer afternoons that had now become so pleasurable, since by tempting the dove with bread crumbs and grains of rice she had managed to lure him into her room. Or was it her blonde hair upon her shoulders, the suggestion of her breasts under her diaphanous nightgowns? And one joyful encounter followed another. They became intimate. Her knight, her enchanted prince, did indeed know how to love. As a dove, sometimes, perched on the footboard of the bed, he watched her intensely, and he was so bewitching that he made her caress herself until he tore from her body the most consummate pleasures. When she came to the paroxysm of pleasure, he took on human form and possessed her, without even taking the trouble to slip off his dark cape and his heavy coat of arms.

"Don't you think, Señora, that you're taking awfully long siestas? Sleeping so much is bad for you, Doña Catalina, it would make anyone go soft in the head. Just look at yourself in the mirror. The bags under your eyes reach to your waist and despite all you eat, forgive me for saying this, you're as thin as a fish bone. What will Don Diego say when he returns and sees you like this? That I didn't know how to take care of you?"

Doña Acacia was right; the mirror cried out this truth when she looked in it.

"What are you saying, woman?" she answered. "What would become of me if not for these siestas that shorten my days here, confined to this bed? And with this damn heat!"

It was true, her daily life crawled along like a pitiful caterpillar from daybreak until early afternoon, when her soul left her breast like a butterfly taking flight. What other delight existed for her besides making love with her handsome, mute knight? Indeed, he was always silent; she had never heard him speak a word. But the delicious brush of his delicate wing-feathers over all the curves of her body, the vigor of his beak delving into her body's most sensitive zones of pleasure, and the way in which he put it in her mouth, to drink from her saliva and play indulgently with her tongue, made up for it all.

"You've spent two weeks in bed already," the servant continued. "The doctor is coming to see you again soon, and he will probably allow you to get up and take a few steps. Ah, and cheer up, because according to my calculations, the return of the ships is not far off and soon you will have Don Diego here, to cajole you."

The servant's comment made Catalina bite her lips to prevent her despair from causing her to curse. No, she no longer needed the presence of her husband or anyone else, but she lied and said how happy she was to hear of her husband's imminent return, thinking all the while, in distress, about what her future life would be like when that lout (as she now called him), would approach her and, even worse, when he would throw his repulsive body on top of hers.

These thoughts kept her occupied all morning. When it was finally time for her siesta, she surrendered to it with the usual fervor. She dozed off wishing for nothing more than the arrival of that moment when she would open her eyes and as if by magic the small, resplendent figure would appear on the wall. She sailed along drenched in sweat, feeling as if the bed were a small white-sailed ship, its lightness contrasting with the dark and heavy furniture that surrounded her, big as galleons and smelling of utter shipwreck. Finally, she opened her eyes and saw the dove shimmering in the sunlight. She watched him take flight and come, once again, to her bed. And as she did every afternoon, she gave him her naked body so that his delightful ashy beak might peck at her taut breasts, her lips, the tangle of hair of her triangle which came to an end in proud flesh of capricious design, and sink into her short tunnel of delights. She reveled in those caresses with more passion than ever before until, reaching the peak of ecstasy and falling from this tension to complete bliss, she watched him leave through tears of joy.

The days went by and she felt that, in comparison with a reality she experienced as vague and insubstantial, as if seen through a veil or heard like the sound of the sea in a shell, only her passion was truly real. Acacia noticed her uneasiness and worriedly shook her head.

"For God's sake, Señora!" she would say. "It's a good thing Don Diego will soon be here, the longing is killing you."

Acacia's words rang true in Catalina's consciousness. She couldn't imagine what repercussions this event would have on her daily rendezvous, although she knew that all the possible conclusions to that adventure were closely linked to the imminent arrival of her lord and master.

The doctor finally paid her a call, just as Acacia had announced. He arrived with mud-covered boots, having been obliged to make his way through the mud-holes of the streets on foot; because the horses' hooves became mired, they were impassable by other means. After carefully examining her leg he said:

"My dear lady, you can get out of bed now, sit in your favorite armchair and even take a few strolls. As long as you don't overdo it, of course!"

It was Doña Acacia who answered him because Catalina was absorbed in thought.

"Thank you, Señor. Don Diego will know how to express his appreciation for your leaving him the Señora healthy and as pretty as ever. He will be very generous, you can be sure."

"I know. Don Diego and I will settle it later."

The doctor and Acacia left the room. Catalina got up by herself and went to sit in an armchair beside the balcony. Seated there, she viewed the familiar ruins from a different angle than she'd contemplated during the two weeks when she had not left her bed. She lifted her gaze until she could make out the coastline where the sea spray fleetingly adorned the coral shore. She looked farther out to the point where the sea and sky appeared to meet, fearing she might spot the shapes of the ships in the distance. She spent hours in this state of anticipation until her despair began to give way to a sense of peace. After all, she was no longer confined to bed. Soon she would ride her stallion again along shady paths born amid the thickness of the nearby woods. She would bathe again, naked, in the pool whose waters were cooled by the shade of huge rocks. She would stroll barefoot through the garden enjoying the morning dew. She would walk caressed by the scent of jasmine and roses and the sharp smell of pomegranates. And she would not give up her afternoon trysts. No. As for her husband, she would submit to all his whims, which after all, had no reason to upset her so much. Besides, she would undoubtedly jump the garden wall again whenever she fancied. Finally she rose from the armchair and went over to the night table where she picked up the little bell to call Doña Acacia, and as she shook it, eliciting its authoritative jingle, she thought about the tasty dinner she would soon devour.

Rosa Ileana Boudet, born 1947, lives in Havana. Her published work from 1977 to 1988 includes the novella *Alánimo, Alánimo*, the oral history *The Little Cowboy*, the essay "New Theater: A Reply," and a book of stories, *This Single Kingdom*. "Potosí 11: Address Unknown" appeared in the 1996 anthology *Pillars of Salt*.

Translated by Cindy Schuster

Potosí 11:
Address Unknown

Perhaps I should have slammed the door like Nora, strident and categorical. I can't get that line out of my head; it plagues my dreams, disquiets me at night. I want to write it down, but I resist my own impulses. I look around me. I have just packed up and moved out of provisional living quarters. My lot as a frequenter of rummage sales and flea markets is over. What has it left in me? Incoherent ramblings. I will continue to be alien to many people. They won't even consider me in literary circles; your work has no genre, get used to it, said the editor, it doesn't work for me. It's like a torrent, said another one, a text full of muscles, juices, and membranes. But I keep at it during the time I steal from my temporary jobs, from the vocation of saucepans, from the drudgery that burdens all women. I don't miss my house or the noise or the loud cries of hawkers in the Chamartín market. I miss walking around alone in order to live my solitary life, and I chart my course in these confessions.

It has been shattering to discover that I invented my characters, my Valentinos, my lovers, and to find out that love is as ephemeral as twenty-four hours in an Old Havana *posada** or a dawn in the Santa Clara Libre Hotel. Unlike Simone, I have yet to find old age in a urine stain on the carpet. But it will come. And then I'll regret not having said *enough* and not flinging the door shut like Nora in the final act.

I come back. I am more alone than ever. I have no heroes or favorite writers. I don't identify with any movie stars. No one will knock on my door (or even call me on the phone) to pay me a compliment. Nobody will dare take me to bed and if they write a dedication, it is a caricature of a past self who was real and convincing. The men who surround me, asexual and androgynous, are attractive mannequins. My generation loved the tough man of the tough times, the rebellious and irascible writer, not the policy-sellers or the providers of consumer goods or the sad public employees. What to do? Where are the rebels of yesteryear? Perhaps the girl playing musical chairs has run long enough. What has she left behind? Yearning.

Yesterday, out of the blue, in a very retro mood, I looked over old photos that my daughter had hidden like spoils of war. I found you by the Las Casas River, with a dedication written in a schoolchild's hand that says, "The Old Man and the River." They were codes: one day Lord Byron, another Licentiate Vidriera. Where

---

* Type of hotel in which rooms are rented by the hour.

are you? Somebody once told me a story of horror and espionage because you had sent me the menu, rustic like everything about you, from the very same tavern where a certain Marlon Brando had filmed *Burn*. Now that years have gone by, the world has changed so much and perhaps I could no longer visit all of Havana's *posadas* with you without embarrassment, I remembered the time when, unpoetically, bluntly and chauvinistically, you said that I would always remember you because of the way you made love. Now that I hardly ever do it, a real kiss from a man gives me goose bumps. I take tranquilizers and I'm not as pretty as you imagined, I know it was true, you were the wise one, old sea dog, dark retired Mig-40 pilot, strange being from an unknown planet who knew how to enter my body at any time, with or without preliminaries. And that sublimated sensation of being a woman returns. Being a woman was the half-light of certain dirty places, soiled sheets and beautiful graffiti on the walls. If I were ever to try it again, to go to bed at dawn with a lord, or a man who sounds like my actor in *Moscow Does Not Believe in Tears* when he swallows his soup, I would be unfaithful by virtue of intimate investigation of my body: how I would respond to those caresses, how I would hold back my orgasm or not, all moist and inflamed by you and you would know, yes, we grew old and it was unforgettable.

I come back to myself. I hide the photo. I would like to go back fifteen years and give myself over to the infinite, send it all to hell so that an insolent look might again devour me. I climb up onto the shrimper while a chorus of dock workers look at the young girl; the wind lifts her skirts. Now I say, how delightful, the writer stopping traffic and disconcerting the provincial girls. I wouldn't be taking all these sleeping pills—they're organic, not barbiturates but just as unpleasant—and I'd be counting the minutes until I met you in some park, because you're here among my trophies, my literary accomplishments, my best lines, in the core of my body.

I feel the solitude of a runner stuck in place, imprisoned in a single repetitive movement. I experience a certain relief when I flee from the blank page, from its yellow texture—I'm running out of paper, the typewriter is defective, the "e" is always incomplete, the letters don't print immaculately on the page—I can always find a pretext to abandon it and feel a twinge of fear, intolerable and ridiculous. But I'm the same person, tenacious, impassioned, determined, who crashes into the same wall. I'm the same person without lovers, without love, without letters. The visitors who interrupt my nights are my daughter's ex-boyfriends who stay until morning creating their Bohemia and looking for a place to harbor their estrangement. Casual friends come looking for some not exactly spiritual thing: a razor blade, a spark plug, a sleeping pill. Will I be able to catalog my pleasures? Who'll cry with me in the night when I tremble at the memory, the allure I can't resist, my sweetheart, since our first true embrace, those classic boleros playing and we'd dance, *cheek to cheek*, touching, holding each other close, the passion you bring from afar oh my love?

The thought of a suspended race brings me back to you. A starting point. A place I can go back to—a murderous look during a boring party—just to regain my old self-confidence, to feel that I return to my space and open myself again to your embrace, older and somewhat tired, but as persistent and hard-pressed as I was when we met and you gave me a ring.

I wake up when my body is ready. I enjoy lounging between the sheets with no schedules and no doorbells. I am wrapped in sheltering blankets and when the sun comes through the curtains, I know the day has begun. I'm forty years old and this is the first time I've ever enjoyed a time all to myself; a time which passes awkwardly and with savage monotony. I wake with no particular obligations and that makes me feel nauseous, a floating island. And I discover that I feel guilty and commit myself to simple tasks so as not to become disconnected from my accustomed role of wage earner. At night, when I can't sleep and the noises of the house grow louder inside my head, I imagine again that I am driving through the narrow streets, that I arrive early at my job, that someone needs me, I get a call, and that curious ritual calms me down. I am myself again. I no longer appropriate someone else's character: I make coffee, take the laundry off the clothesline, dust the furniture, mop the floor, heat up yesterday's rice. And in each one of these acts—a cruel chain—I am not myself, but someone else, while the one taking my place out there rushes through the streets, occupied with other hapless routines, pressed for time but enjoying life more, beset by emergencies.

When I depict my apathetic character here in bed, listless between the sheets, indolent and silly, I am undoubtedly miserable. I don't know what will become of me, lonely as an astronaut in the dark night of space, when all the answering machines say *wrong number.* No one will believe that I haven't enjoyed Cibeles, or the warm nocturnal city, or wandering through the galleries of the Prado attracting compliments. Be that as it may, my daughter, I know that you'll make a beautiful Ophelia, with your hair slicked down and wet like the silent movie stars, that you'll sing her mysterious madness, arrogant like the real ones, rebellious like the divas who, absent and pale from cold, have crossed all the stages repeating their lines and bringing the ceremony back to life.

I feel myself fighting this celebration of my forty years. The gypsy on the corner has not come with his sad boleros and his repertoire intact. Unexpected sounds, tangos played on a hand or-gan, may interrupt the silence. I am, as always, inside my oyster. I have constructed my habitat from ashes, certain of where the four cardinal points lie.

My daughter: I will never be a worldly woman. The other day, in television city, I finally discovered who Garfunkel was. Like Oliver and Hardy, he was inseparable from Simon, and I must admit the poor country boy disappointed me, with his syrupy voice that at one time may have been all the rage, I won't deny you that. And Madonna, that fabrication who tries to pass for an easily domesticated puppy. But it's all a lie, because on TV a city can defy you with its invisible and civilized arteries, even if you get bored with conversations with the same friends, drinking the same beer and the same rum.

The air acquires a sleepy intimation, your bones ache in the mornings, your period arrives punctually as an old lady and among the shop windows sparkling with seductive fashions, you feel as without a "look" as a kitchen-maid, as ugly as the scrub-woman, as sexless as a corpse. So you try to turn heads again, go back to your old self, slow down your pace, turn off the TV inundated with commercials and raise your eyes toward the Malecón de Cádiz, covered with posters that say CHE CHE CHE, painted with LONG LIVE MAGIC MARXISM, and macho Andalusians sitting at the bars finishing off a sherry. And a brilliant, magnificent Costa del Sol and towns white enough to vanquish all of one's sleepless nights.

But the night becomes endless when the image of that huge flea market, the *Rastro*, haunts you, that sad garbage dump where so much despair, disgust, and estrangement is deposited: objects thrown in the mud, bitter, weather-beaten faces, so different from the ones in the shopwindows on the Gran Vía. It's the Puerta de Toledo. Swarms of people go looking for a secondhand or stolen article of clothing, that smells of alcohol or nicotine, that sweats rage, or pornographic or horrific magazines that have passed through elusive hands, withered furs, unusual objects—a disturbing yet seductive antique shop where a woman chances upon her first coat, out of style but elegant, fresh from a lady's closet, a luminous Sunday miracle.

The desolate *Rastro* does not humiliate you. Deep down you are happier with your woolen inverness than in Beatriz's fur shop where the skins of foxes, sheep, and other animals teach you to look at yourself differently in the mirror, to incorporate another self in front of the dressing room where you take turns with a French woman in a wig and astrakhan, like those painted by Toulouse-Lautrec, posh ladies with credit cards and charge accounts who change their furs every season, old ladies in wheelchairs who long for a new wrap. And you watch them go by like an entertaining prologue. You prefer your gray wool coat, the color of smoke, that the gypsy pulled out for you like a bird from her hat.

Because you've always had birds in your head—and muscles, juices and fibers—as a certain writer in the twilight of his glory, albeit a tender night owl, told you. And maybe it's because of those birds that hovered around you that you can't sleep; you're assailed by the lines of an inconclusive letter or the interview you couldn't finish, and because of that the breathing of the one sleeping next to you becomes enormous as a highway, cavernous as an illness, while you try to break through into the uncertainty of dawn. And the thing is, you're flooded with birds in the Reina Sofía where Miró's huge canvases are revelations of woman mixed with birds in childlike, unsettling brush strokes, poppy-stained surfaces, tailor's and dressmaker's patterns, so much imagination, so much tenderness. And you go down Moyano Hill with his world on your shoulders, a world so compatible with yours, so easy to understand and protect. Maybe I recognized myself in that woman in a trance looking out at the shooting stars. Women in Miro's work reappear as do birds. I'm forty years old. I never get tired of walking around the gallery in my worn-out clothes. I don't profess to be anything other than myself, my daughter, retracing an interminable journey from my interior landscape.

In the morning I rummaged through the bookstore like someone gobbling candies. I prepared a frugal lunch for an equally anxious guest who brought chocolates for dessert. The scene at the corner of Colón was bathed in sunlight, fit for a photograph, the books out of reach. And I had to repress my desires, wring out time, live on past glories and sleep. Except that when a woman doesn't sleep it's usually because she's watching over someone else or getting up to take care of them, or because she has a fever and is tormented by boredom. There are so many reasons that I thought this time I was suffering from insomnia, and that crazy, taciturn Miró-birds had been let loose over my head.

The noises that penetrate Potosí's opaque windows—the alarms, the shriek of ambulances, and the honking of trucks—are not like the racket in my neighborhood, the din of the junkyard, and water flooding the drains. It's the noise of the big city with its punches and blows greeting me with a sullen look. A sound dispersed in the air like gunpowder and soot.

To arrive at Potosí is to inhabit an impersonal hotel. Others have lived here without leaving a trace, not even a stain on the easy chair or the moan of a heart attack in the rocker. Nobody bothered to replace the pictures of galloping horses in their shining frames, or the pictures of galleons or the sea either. A choppy sea, garnished with a red border, a gold-plated mirror like my mother's furniture. To go out on the balcony is to see the street and some sad flower-beds with pale dirt. To return to the house is to trip over my own silhouette reflected in the shining wood and to remember my Mendive, my cheeks, my ferns, the bewitched quantity of my age. It is to return to my self, lost in this damn city or humiliated when a phony gypsy, with pitiful sweetness, recites me a future of travel and happiness by the edge of the pool in the Retiro. She insulted me because she thought my handout insufficient. Fortune-telling has its price. The ability to read destiny in the lines of your palm is a commodity. I don't know what I could possibly have said to poor Julius that was so important to him. I followed the trail of the old usurer who, like a bad actress, repeated her predictions to others with exactly the same words. I walked to the Ibiza station, got off at Pío XII, frightened. The old woman's face was my sullen welcome.

Have I lost my memory? Yesterday, during a long nocturnal vigil, I tried to reconstruct that seedy hotel where the manager knocked loudly on our door and the spell was broken. But the man never materialized; nor did we appear in search of a room after walking all over town for hours, visiting wharves, amusement parks, fountains and squares, like two ill-fated lovers lost in the labyrinth of Havana, trapped by its columns and tiles, two incredible wanderers who sat down to talk in El Templete and watch the ships in the harbor. My sensations evaporated along with my memory. I could recall neither the caresses nor the kisses. This sounds ridiculous, but it is precise. I write it and tremble. Undressing was a celebration and being penetrated was an intense dialogue that ended inside me like a concert, an arrow, a small death or a birth. I felt beautiful in your arms, a lover, energetic and loved, even if it wasn't true. The *posadas* were a backdrop and the noises a celestial accompaniment; the act of surrender aroused new passions and unleashed hidden feelings, that had been repressed by the foul-smelling, sordid scab of loneliness. Am I not more lonely when I'm with a man? I tried to reconstruct the route to the *posada* where someone waited for me but I couldn't seem to take a step, cross a street corner, recognize the bus stop or the address. My senses are atrophying. The smells of onion, garlic, and spices superimposed themselves over those of a naked body, the acrid sweat of a man and the warmth of his arms. In their place I smelled the insipid perfume of the packed-up home, vapid tears, and I woke up horrified at not having been able to find the bus stop we used to rush to, beautiful as two sentries, so sure of ourselves and so much the masters of our destiny. The shipwreck of insomnia became a ghost at dawn. I noticed that I was incapable of daydreaming, of recovering smells and branding moments for eternity.

In those days I used to walk around in sandals. I didn't want you forever, but loved you with the intense transience of a challenge, with a taste for loss and reunion, for risk on the high seas. The sea played a dirty trick on us and he who signed telegrams as Lord Byron and sent them to a so-called Licentiate Vidriera, in reality set sail forever without farewells or poems. And now that I have twelve hours of true refuge at my disposal, this night of solitude, I can barely remember where we were, neither the days nor the dates, if a gust of wind messed up my hair or not, or even the persistent smell of the sheets where I went to bed with you. That was happiness. I remember. The happiness of letting oneself be carried along like an invalid restored to health across walkways and isolated spots. The happiness of being a woman. The happiness of sharing that piece of bed and window, of opening the door up wide and leaving that miserable *posada* certain that we had realized a singular, incredible, and fleeting conquest.

At the onset (that's how you put it) generally there isn't much left of a woman and she doesn't get bored. At the onset one endures many anxious hours, a novel is a revelation, one goes to bed at dawn and wakes as if she had slept, it doesn't matter, at least she dreams; she watches over his breathing and waits for daybreak in the Edén Abajo. She doesn't care what people think, gathered around a Mongolian contortionist or the light of four candles and a *feeling** singer; at this stage a woman doesn't mind seeing the worst movie in the world because one can always make fun of the singers or the waiters, balk at the outrageous bill that appears at an inopportune moment, laugh sadly at "Aurora My Life" or Cristina, embarrassed and proper. Rather, at this stage she goes through life hoarding sensations in order to spill them out later when she's with you; that's it, a woman in love buys cheap cognac and invents intrigues without rituals and special ceremonies. At the onset dance halls spark conversations, highways light up, and at night amusement park rides frighten and thrill those who play at being children. And boleros, boleros are pleasing too in the sleepy night, making fun of *Captain Pantoja and the Special Service*, pretend someone's holding you tight and a firm hand grips your waist and you feel that you need for that hand to stay there. At the onset I take the tropical path and in the elusive shadow of José Antonio there are bohemian gatherings and sold-out movies. Demba's singing breaks your heart at the onset, one likes meetings and fighting for one's idea of justice so that later when the cats come to eat from our scraps in Bellomonte, you earnestly insist that you're right, you're almost always right or we both are, no one dares lay claim to the absolute truth, but neither does it all transpire in perfect harmony, the discord continues, the rhythm of skin growing wrinkled, one looks in the mirror and says time is passing my woman 'til death . . . And ve-

---

* A ballad form of music evolved from the bolero.

locity sweeps me up, one idealizes things, after all is said and done
it's worth it to love you, no ceremony can compare to that of waking with the knowledge that a tear weighs you down, that bells
toll, that you quiver with emotion in a letter, just don't let it die,
that's all I ask. At the onset one hardly speaks, one whispers,
trembles, the proxemics and kinesics of flirtation and courtship
come into play, the couples in line at the Edén, the paradise of
nonverbal language, at that stage one does not drift but is in a
state of belonging, strange personal property of knowing that one
belongs to another when someone gets undressed and breathes
and is cold or simply wants to turn and go. At the onset one does
not count the days, time is not wasted, one doesn't check the calendar; only when the onset has passed and life goes on as usual do
these things happen.

What will come to pass tomorrow blue Saturday bright Sunday? Without the noise of the house and the chores to do, the voice
of Embale stirs me. I feel more at ease, like one who savors her
own shell. His voice, as he sings *guaguancó*, reminds me of your
friends, your harbor buddies with their dark-skinned girls and
their cold beers singing *feeling* and José Antonio and I won't go to
Santiago at night and all the other things the delights of Liv Ull-
man would bring about. Nonetheless, I am here alone again, with
a desire to run but with no destination, fretting over everyday concerns, consoling myself with my Brandenburg concertos and your
sailor's hands and your despair and your very special obscenities
and your liters of rum and your beer because yes, it's true what
Tovstonogov says, the public today is more interested in interior
processes, this will be a success, a bestseller, a look into my guts,
liver, and kidneys, an unburdening dedicated to you in two voices.

That face of yours was a poem in that strange assembly in Gerona, you in military dress, unshaven, shining like a street lamp

and surprisingly vapid to me who remembered you haranguing people at the University and drawing applause in the Arts School theater. Was I one of those women who were born with you? I wasn't a fellow traveler, I wasn't even a muse, neither was I an incorrigible beauty, nor the playful alchemy of the song book. I was fulfilling my duty there from one island to another,* but I can't forget your face among the multitude in that interior island like the fire in the Plaza Cadenas, or from before, when we kids invaded the immaculate neighborhoods of the bourgeoisie with the lifestyles of peasants and workers. Aurora wouldn't be your proletarian girl, nor would the rare virgin, or a cheap woman either, because the unmistakable face is never erased, Alí la Fuent, Vallejo's poems, Vallejo's rain reminding us that we were a sorry lot, had it not been for the Revolution that put us all under the same mosquito net, touching another shore, closer to each other.

The city lights grow faint and those who were born with me wander, grow wary and bitter, betray you, and I am left with Mozart's strings for company while I dust the furniture and scrub the floor, the moldings, the china, the battered bottoms of the saucepans, with heroic force. Everything disintegrates in ferocious routine. And how to escape, how to journey toward those stirrings if my memories slip away? Over there are the dishes, my daughter's sketch of a flower, the flag, the watercolor, Alice through the looking-glass, I don't know what's happening to me but I have a feeling, I do know what's happening to me, the air has a blue smell like the horizon we never saw together. Almost no one will understand this provincial confession today, this letter written through the night by a Portuguese nun with neither officer nor army. Silvio Rodriguez sings his testament and Rubén Blades's salsa belatedly shakes out the afternoon, rinsed clean by the rain. You always

---

* Gerona is on the Isle of Youth, a small island off the coast of Cuba.

said that rain was associated with my memory and out of this sense of loyalty, I think it's raining in that grotto of the mirror that separates us, as if it were always a sense of relief that I feel when I no longer have you. The damp air smells like earth. Water washes the street. And I remember you now, dirty and scratched up, your shoes on the doorstep, while I stroked my skin, now that I wish I could go back to the onset and laugh again at those trivial things.

It fills me with pity that a man would gamble against infinity on his knees before two nipples and a clitoris. I was astonished that he appeared before the TV cameras like a defunct infant,* that once-colossal charmer, enveloped in a parodic poncho, who besieged me with flirtatious remarks on a Havana street when miniskirts were in fashion and the infant described me as the scandal of the provincial girls. Now the infant speaks a translated Spanish, he calls the chicks and the babes girls, and ties all his sentences together with a ridiculous "For God's sake." Now he wears a suit and tie, repeats old myths and obsessions with wearisome indifference. He leaves his London apartment sadly, confesses with reckless pride that he has undergone eighteen electroshock treatments as he chews on his proverbial *puro*, a prodigious cigar, with the insolence of the nobody from Gibara despite his elegant and casually studied manners. He read a book by Dashiell Hammett and came across a forgotten Fritz Lang movie in his video library by chance, his cat died, his wife is convalescing from a sudden grave illness, and he believes that nostalgia is the whore of memory and refuses to do business with such a lady. I turn on the TV and see before me—twenty-five years ago—that arrogant mulatto whose words set me on fire as I reached the end of my

---

* Guillermo Cabrera Infante, Cuban writer in exile, born in the town of Gibara, author of *La Habana para un infante difunto* (*Infante's Inferno*) and *Tres tristes tigres* (*Three Trapped Tigers*).

route to the Wakamba nightclub. La Rampa was the favorite gathering place for young people, my daughter, and my memory of the infant dates back to a brief moment, a long street and as I'm crossing 23rd, that pompous ass asks me to leave my skirt alone, don't touch it, it whipped around in the gale-force wind. The infant turned into a dissident, he manufactured a custom-made madness, frivolous cineaste, scholar of the thriller and the erotic, he got himself elegant clothes and turned himself into a character. On the screen I saw someone out of a book. I was no longer the schoolgirl assailed with ineffable flirtatious remarks who was going to walk the Rampa just for the fun of it, capable of conquering the world and the infant. I am sitting in front of a myth that breaks apart just like the Beatles got old and stars commit suicide. But I felt an inexpressible sadness, like that of a trapped tiger when I saw the infant—now pushing sixty—chewing his cigar with exemplary Cubanism, graying and haughty, talking with uncommon audacity about the size of the penis of a kangaroo who flirted with him in an Australian zoo. The provincial, bewildered by his travels, could find nothing better to tell the television audience about than that putrid memory of his flirtation with a marsupial from Adelaide.

His boleros, his vignettes of love and war, his pseudonyms and games, his particular brand of "non sense" are left behind; his Josefina attends to the gentlemen in their every need, even their incredible farts which, since our bodies are not divine, inopportunely interrupt their coitus; left behind as if in a thick fog are the Indian adorned in his poncho, the sarcastic, daring Don Juan, the proprietor of paths and flirtatious comments for budding girls like me. You certainly don't belong here, my dear infant, you really are from the nineteenth century, you are writing itself and you will remain like tireless writing that tries to take control of something you're not—that gives itself away in the angry *puro* you've chewed to a shred—as you furiously and avidly devour it.

I turn off the TV, I pass the time watching the snow, the flakes falling on the roof. I begin to sing old tangos and from time to time I remember the other one, another possibly defunct infant who consumed a night with a bottle of seven-year-old Havana Club, while he had no idea what to do with two nipples and a clitoris that watched him from a hotel room.

Every time the face of Jean Pierre Leaud appears on the screen with its unmistakable tic and its kiss-stealing grimaces, I see your image. You are in that gang of disapproved of and frightened naughty little boys who got a zero for conduct, and I follow you from my window as if the sixties were our glory and our nightmare. Your face supplants the playful and tolerant gaze of the actor on camera. You too tried to play at film, practice beautiful tracking shots, and experiment with risky zooms, your conversations were full of film, real film in big capital letters, riddled with quotations from innumerable scenes; your love was also very cinematic. Your declarations were very Lorca and Baudelaire, Ionesco, and Horacio Quiroga. We wanted to be damned and angry young beats. Or maybe Camus-like existentialists as well, wild neorealists in the shadow of Zavattini. And you needed the presence of a certain young woman everywhere you went, not as sex but as poetry. You insisted on that phrase. She frequented shadowy places, talked about stories of the dead, jungles and big feather pillows; she smoked. I could never understand what I was doing in that adolescent triangle and what you meant by it wasn't sex but poetry. When I'd see her at your side, beautiful and mysterious, casting you furtive glances, I'd feel the curl of cigarette smoke, the air pitching upwards while a saxophone chased down magnificent notes. It was the Malecón and the sea was pounding,

I was too young to understand you then and I was frightened by your muse of horrific and savage stories, I who yearned to be your sex and your poetry.

Jean Pierre's face reminds me of you. I'm obsessed with the idea of what would have become of me had I consummated my first love. And I see myself thunderstruck when I heard that voice say: "My parents are taking me away from Cuba. I'm leaving you." Laconic and false, it seemed like a dialogue from some atrocious melodrama. And I thought about the stranger who knew about it all along, who was there until the end, at the last good-bye. What would have become of us? I would have missed my finest moment, my first love which time has sublimated and which lingers in a warm, run-down room. The secretly imagined love of a girl who looked around her and sensed a fleeting warning in the melody of a saxophone. I never saw you again. You are in this room, in my manuscript, in this letter to an address unknown.

Or perhaps here again now in Charlie Parker, who pursues you as well as me, the celebrity you enjoy in your remote exile. A serene, mournful, and macabre pursuer. Or you could be sitting here next to me and we would have nothing to say to each other, reflecting upon the long walks we used to take, remembering the long-legged girl who existed in your heart only as poetry. The sea from the horizon. That tender lacerating spell that made me weep, when I realized that she existed for you and that I was always a precocious, but impossible burst of passion. Never again. Always. You reappear each night in the face of Jean Pierre Leaud.

Sonia Rivera-Valdés, born in 1937, has lived in New York since the 1960s. Currently a professor at York College, she writes in Spanish and has published her stories in various literary magazines in the United States. "A Whiff of Wild Desire" comes from her story collection *The Forbidden Tales of Marta Veneranda*, winner of the Casa de las Américas prize.

Translated by Dick Cluster

A Whiff of Wild Desire

Now that I'm here I don't know where to start. I'm afraid of telling it and having you think I'm crazy—or worse, that I'm a pig—but if I don't tell somebody I'll end up truly beyond the beyond, and maybe I'll find it easier with you, ma'am, precisely because I don't know you and I'll probably never see you again. And besides, if as Mayté says, you've spent more than two years hearing people tell you things they haven't dared to say to another soul, well, maybe my story won't seem so weird, because God knows what else you've heard. Mayté's own story is pretty crazy, in truth. But mine is worse. I swear it.

No, don't worry about that. If I can summon up the courage to tell you, I don't care if you publish it. As long as you don't mention my name, of course. This story is so strange and different from what my life has been like up till now, that nobody's going to recognize me in it. For it to happen to me is truly strange, because I'm so committed to cleanliness that I'll take a bath even if I'm running a fever of a hundred and four. You're Cuban, you know the fixation we Cubans have about smells. For us, stinking is a capital crime. Who that knows me is going to think I did what I did? Nobody. Not even my wife would believe it, and I've lived with her for more than ten years.

I'm going to tell you the whole truth. I came here because Mayté insisted so much, and I feel so . . . I don't know . . . let's say . . . disconcerted, disturbed, messed up, who knows. The thing is that, because I can't manage to forget this shit—and pardon the bad language—she told me that I had to at least give you a try. Maybe this conversation can somehow get it all off my mind, like what happened to her with all that about Laura, because according to what she says, telling it relieved her like magic, and I know pretty well how heavily that thing was weighing on her. But let me tell you, my first reaction when she suggested this was to reject it 100 percent. How could she think that I was going to tell somebody I didn't even know about something that I can't spit out even to the people closest to me like Mayté herself? You can imagine how I feel. Look at me, sitting here talking to you. I've told Mayté things I never told Miguel, who's been my friend since we were little, we went to the beach together every day, back in Jaimanitas. Miguel, who thanks to life's twists and turns is here living in New York now too.

But what brought me to see you, not for the life of me am I going to tell it to either of them. What happened is that Mayté knows me too well, we've been working together for years at the paper, and she saw right away that something was eating at me, though at first I denied it and told her that I was just tired, that nothing was going on. Imagine, me, with my reputation for writing with ease, I've been waiting till the last minute to crank out my articles, and writing them badly too. It takes such an effort for me to concentrate, and even to speak coherently. Look at this conversation I'm having with you, that hasn't got any beginning or end. Normally I'm an articulate individual, and well-mannered too.

Sure, I know a therapist. I not only know one, I've been going to one for a long time. I know I could go see him, I've thought about it a lot, but no way, I'm not telling this to him. I'd die first, from the shame of him knowing about this. After all these years, we're friends, don't you see? He'll think I've gone crazy if he hears this string of nutty things. Believe me. He's known me since I was fifteen, fresh from Cuba. It was because of an obsession I was having about the beach at Jaimanitas, where I lived until I was fourteen.

Yes, that's how it was, with Operation Peter Pan.* That operation screwed up so many people.

My father above all. Fear, no, terror that I'd get taken for military service, and he didn't think about it twice. No, the whole family was still there. They came here a year later. Did I have a hard time? Real hard. I don't want to remember. But the thing was that while I was alone I didn't think about anyone but them, and then, as soon as they got here and I had a more or less normal family again, I started to miss this girlfriend I'd left behind at the

---

* Operation Peter Pan, organized by church and exile groups in the early 1960s, brought fifteen thousand unaccompanied Cuban children to the United States as refugees from alleged communist control over their upbringing. They were placed with foster families or relatives.

beach. A lovely girl. I liked her, you can't imagine how much. And I got to thinking, but I mean thinking day and night, an obsession like in the movies, that was the problem, that every afternoon she was going with another guy to the same bridge where we two used to go, to watch the sun set, the last few months that I lived there. Now it seems incredible that I could have suffered so much for such a silly thing, but at that point I practically gave up eating for days at a time.

It was a bridge by the sea, over some coral. Wooden, small, and half ruined by the surf. Hardly anybody used it and the bottom was full of shellfish. But I was a boy, and for me those afternoons were the most beautiful in the world, leaning against the rail of the bridge, hugging the girl with my arm around her waist. They were glorious, ma'am, glorious.

The psychologist helped me out a lot and finally I got over my depression. It's been a while since I've seen him, and he thinks I'm in as good shape as can be. And really, I was, until this happened. No way . . . I'm not going to tell him. Look, I've been all over it in my mind, over and over, and I can't find any explanation. Two months now, and I still think about it when I get up and think about it when I go to bed. I'm much worse than I was about Jaimanitas, much worse.

Yes, I know I'm going around in more circles than a spinning top, of course I know that. But it's such an effort to get started.

It was a Saturday morning. Iris had left early to see her mother in New Jersey and wasn't going to be back until late. She took the girl with her. Around ten I was getting ready to sit down and read, happy about the idea of few hours peace and quiet, when somebody knocked on the door. It seemed strange because almost no one knocks on the apartment door without us having to open the downstairs lobby door first. I looked through the peephole and, before I could see who it was, I heard a woman's voice saying that something terrible had happened. It was the neighbor from the apartment next door. I opened up, and she said all in a rush that it was an emergency. She'd been straightening up the house for its weekend cleaning and filling the bathtub for her bath. She went out in the corridor with a ton of old newspapers to put them next to her door so she could take them down to the recycling bin in the basement later on, when, suddenly, the door closed and locked behind her. Nobody in the building had an extra key to her apartment. Once a friend across the street had one, but he'd moved not long before, and the super lives out on Long Island. And, to top it off, she'd been about to get in the bath at the moment when her door shut, so when she knocked on mine she was wasn't wearing anything but a T-shirt which barely reached to the tops of her enormous thighs—because my neighbor weighs about four hundred pounds. No, I'm not exaggerating, she's that immensely fat. My only dealings with her had been mutual greetings when we met in the hallways or elevators, but often enough Iris and I had watched her morning trip from apartment to elevator, through the peephole of our door. Because her weight astonished us, and what also caught our attention was the way she walked, swaying from one side to the other.

I asked her to come in. She entered swaying, and the thin cloth of the T-shirt let me see the heaping balls of fat that hung under her arms, around her hips, from her thighs. Her chestnut hair was loose and her light gray eyes shone almost transparently. I'd never seen her so close up. A very pretty face, smooth skin, slightly thick lips, and straight white teeth. I went to the kitchen to rummage in a drawer for the emergency phone number, to get ahold of someone from the building's maintenance department who would take care of the situation. If we couldn't contact anyone, then we'd call a locksmith.

That's when the part that's hard to tell started. When she

closed the door behind her and started toward the living room
couch, a horrible, fetid odor burst into the apartment. I won't try
to describe it, because I've tried, mentally, all this time, and I
haven't been able to. Very strong. The strongest odor I've ever
smelled in my life. A little sour and kind of salty, maybe like shellfish rotting along the edge of a beach after they've been in the sun
for several days. At first I only smelled it, without thinking, but as
the stench grew, the further in she came, I thought it must have
been in my head. It couldn't come from my neighbor, a woman
with a normal apartment, a job, some friends who came to visit.
But when she sat down and I got close to her, to give her the phone
book so she could find a locksmith—since the super turned out to
be impossible to reach—I was convinced that in fact she was giving off a fearful stink. She hadn't bathed in at least a week. I was
nauseous, I swear, that's how strong the smell was. The whole situation seemed unreal, as if I were watching a movie or something.
She finished her phone call and reported that the locksmith was
busy on another emergency at the moment, but he'd be there in
half an hour to help out. Half an hour, I thought. I didn't know if
I could stand it. I didn't want to be inhospitable, though.

I sat down across from her in an armchair, instead of next to
her on the couch, while I tried to pretend that my nose didn't exist
and to ignore the heaves that would come up from my stomach to
my throat every time I forgot to forget the stench.

We started to talk about how wrong it was not to have a super-
intendent living in the building, and from that we moved on to
celebrating how lucky it was that all the neighbors on the sixth
floor got along so well. The stink emanating from that woman invaded the room. She was leaning back against the back of the
couch now, with her legs half open; they were impossible to close
because of the diameter of her thighs. At first I tried not to breathe

with my normal regularity, but caught between suffocating myself or inhaling the rotten sea creatures I felt myself submerged
among—well, I decided to breathe. I listened to the rhythm and
intonation of the sound which came out of her mouth, without
paying attention to the words. By the time ten minutes had gone
by I couldn't hear anymore. All my energy was dedicated to getting through this ordeal.

All of a sudden, her expression grew more meaningful. It didn't
match the triviality of the conversation anymore. Her big gray
eyes, locked on mine, didn't blink. Her eyes and mouth sent me
different messages. She kept on talking in a low, warm tone—because she had a lovely voice, too.

Then, the weirdest thing in the world happened. All of a sudden
I realized I was breathing as hard as I could. I don't mean normally, but with all my lungs, like in a yoga exercise. The stench
was gone, transformed into a deep aroma that I was avid to
breathe in. Leaning back languidly on the couch, her thighs more
open now, the woman was displaying the dark sex that gave off
that intoxicating odor, because that was where the powerful fragrance was welling from. And I didn't think anymore. I don't
know which of my faculties quit functioning, but all of a sudden
we stopped talking and I was staring openly at her shadowy cave
and breathing in that odor, breathing deep. I wanted to sink into
it, wanted it to envelop and devour me. With effort, she shifted position a few times, then spread her legs completely and the folds
of her open vulva blew out a perfume that now entranced me. I
went wild. She fell back on the sofa and pulled up the T-shirt with
her hands, which exposed her gigantic breasts and the three hundred pounds of flesh that surrounded them. I went nuts, I swear
that I went nuts. Wild. Nothing like this had ever happened to me.
The only sane thing I managed to do, thank God, was to get a con-

dom out of the desk drawer where I always keep a few in case Iris and I get a sudden notion while we're watching television after the girl is asleep, and I put it on. There wasn't any romance. And listen, I'm a romantic type, even in the most difficult situations: I told you the story about Jaimanitas. But this was a whole other thing. I went to her with my pants down, before I could finish taking them off. I climbed on top of her and penetrated her—slowly at first, but then strong and savage. She let it happen. She took me soft and open, and so big there on the couch that she couldn't fit and her flesh hung off the edge and, in the middle of all that, I was trying to grab hold so she wouldn't fall on the floor. I sank into her body. That fragrance was all around me, and the more I smelled, the more I wanted to smell more. My nose explored her whole body, searching out the most hidden places, the ones with the strongest smell where the accumulated fat made labyrinths of skin. Can you imagine this?

Really, it didn't last ten minutes. When the locksmith called on the intercom, I jumped off the couch. She lowered her T-shirt, I opened the door, and while she was walking to her apartment she thanked me for the hospitality.

When I went back in my apartment and closed the door, I came to my senses and almost fainted from the nauseating stink. I lit incense and opened the windows even though it was below zero out. The smell abated, but I couldn't read, thinking about what had happened. In the afternoon I made arroz con pollo with a lot of garlic and olive oil, to soak the apartment in those odors before Iris got home. But as soon as she came in, she asked what smelled so strange. I said it was probably the mixture of incense and spices. "Maybe," she said, "but it smells like the ocean to me."

The next morning, when we opened the door to get the newspaper, we found three splendid pears and a thank-you note signed by our neighbor. I told Iris how she'd ended up in the hallway with no keys and I'd helped her take care of the problem. Every now and then I run into her, and we greet each other with that same impersonal cordiality as we did before she got locked out, but I haven't stopped being mortified by all that.

Tell me, ma'am, how would you explain the fact that somebody like me, who's never been able to stand the smell of sweat, should enjoy one that's so much worse? How far would I have gone if the locksmith hadn't arrived? That's what worries me the most. In the end, one doesn't know what one is capable of, given certain circumstances. If it weren't for the condom, which I kept and I look at now and then, I'd think it was a nightmare.

Why do I keep it? I don't know. I just don't know.

Mirta Yáñez, born 1947, has written fiction, poetry, literary criticism, and children's books, and has taught Latin American literature at the University of Havana. In 1988 and 1990 she won the Critics' Prize for the story collection *Go Figure* (which included "Dust to Dust") and for the essay *Romantic Narrative in Latin America*, respectively. Other works published in Cuba include the *The Hour of the Mameys* (a novel, 1984), and *The Visits and Other Poems* (1986). She is the co-editor of the anthology of Cuban women's stories *Pillars of Salt*, published by the Cuban National Union of Writers and Artists in 1996.

Translated by Dick Cluster

Dust to Dust

for Ezequiel Vieta
for Mario Matamoros

In thirty-some years they'd never been separated. Therefore it was easy for Carmela to read the truth in Conchita's face, to feel it as she was hit by one, two, three waves of pain. Beginning to rock furiously in the armchair, she thought a sob was going to escape. But she recovered, the instant that she heard Conchita speak. Conchita, the fool, would not be satisfied if any aspect of the affair was left obscure.

"She had an emergency operation this morning."

Carmela observed her severely, chin thrust forward in that old expression of reproach which the three of them knew so well. Too many years together (and without mixing among "the riffraff," as Conchita said with a disdainful motion of her right shoulder). How many blows of fate had disturbed the flow of their lives. First the hurricane of '32, when the tidal wave had caught them; the damned coincidence, while all three of them were visiting Agustina's family. That was simply indescribable, though Conchita always enjoyed repeating, over and over, the most hair-raising or ridiculous details of the calamity. (Do you remember . . . ?) That was her specialty: to retain from the past only the anecdotes that the rest of the inhabitants of the universe would prefer to forget. But what mattered the most was that they were friends and nothing could separate them.

At that time, Agustina had lost everything, her family had turned into paupers overnight. Which explained how she'd come to live in Carmela's neighborhood. Conchita had grumbled: how would they survive among the hoi polloi? But it was written that they'd all be neighbors. Because next came Conchita's turn. So much dough stored up and, without a peep of warning, financial crisis, down went the government of Machado, horns and all. A venerable politician like the patriarch of Conchita's house (lawyer, businessman, and miser) never could have stood it. Instead he had the bright idea of hanging himself (in a closet, if you can believe that). The dazzling grand piano, where Conchita executed (truthfully speaking she murdered them, well, pounded them, Carmela corrected herself) those Chopin waltzes, greeted one ill-fated dawn out on the street with all its springs, strings, and hammers shamelessly exposed. They had cried together, stamped their feet, lit candles to all the saints, and even offered a glass of water to the spirits. Still and all, the orphan had had no alternative but to set herself up in the same neighborhood as Agustina and Carmela (although much to her grumbling regret). To be near the girls, she'd said, but she was disposed to move as soon as "the situation improved." She'd never done it. No matter how many years (and they were many) Conchita had been threatening to move somewhere else, Carmela had never taken her seriously. How could she stand the loneliness, the distance from her only, closest friends?

Until along came Carmela's own time to face misfortune. No less than a revolution, and menopause on top of that. She wasn't sure how she'd avoided going crazy when they nationalized the small apartment building on Concordia Street. Her only relative (her nephew Alfonso the good-for-nothing) proposed getting out of Cuba. No sir, no. She'd never liked the cold, or even Coca-Cola. She was sensible enough not to run that kind of risk. Her bank account was full (fuller than her friends supposed), her monthly pension high, and she felt comfortable here in the neighborhood. And besides, she had Conchita and Agustina.

Carmela ceased her rocking and diverted her gaze to an indeterminate dark point in space. She breathed noisily through her nose and slapped her palms against the arms of the chair in a brusque gesture that was supposed to show resignation (or perhaps resolution or energy, she herself couldn't tell).

Conchita, for her part, thought that the worst was past. Now she didn't need to clarify anything. She didn't have to say those words that seemed so odious, so indelicate. Much less to get so worked up. To whom would it occur to put together definitive phrases in a normal tone of voice, on such a common, ordinary middle of the day? Conchita had always taken for granted that the subject of death required some preparation. An appropriate atmosphere. And there was none of that on the sunlit front porch at one in the afternoon in a noisy, hurly-burly neighborhood like this (Conchita had always wanted to move, but she'd never found the strength to do so, never the true strength). The buses careening past the corner, the little kids screaming, the radio of the upstairs neighbors (or their television, or their record player, what difference did it make) playing at top blast. No, it was impossible to speak about Agustina's death.

Conchita was still standing, kneading her handkerchief in her hands. She had her change in one of the corners. How this custom disgusted Carmela! Why couldn't Conchita use a change purse like everybody else? The ways she had! Carmela didn't feel in the mood to offer her any consoling words.

Conchita also thought, although for other reasons, that words were completely beside the point. Nonetheless (she couldn't avoid it) she said:

"Not even the Chinese doctor can save Agustina now."

Carmela stopped the motion of the chair. Her sadness had completely disappeared. She looked at Conchita and remembered when she'd seen her arrive for the first time, accompanied by Agustina. In those days they were two skinny, haggard, listless girls. Agustina had stayed that way, skeletal, but Conchita now weighed around two hundred pounds. Something frightening, if you stopped to think it over calmly: more than thirty years growing fatter day by day and hoping for a husband who never appeared. Carmela—first their seamstress, later confidant and friend, and sewing for them always, in good times and bad—had needed summer after summer to increase Conchita's dress size. Agustina's size never varied, but this didn't keep her from being a spinster as well. Carmela was another matter. She married, was widowed, and if she grew old without children it was God's will because (for sure) she had tried often enough. Now she was at peace. Conchita felt a pang of hunger before Carmela's impassive face.

"I'm going to make coffee," Conchita announced, stepping into the shaded passage. Carmela heard her messing with pots in the kitchen, and finally felt calm when she heard the burbling of the liquid. That's done, she said, now we can think with some clarity here.

Conchita returned with two full cups. Before she reached the porch, one of her feet caught on the broken base of the doorframe (thirty-some years tripping over the same place, thought Carmela, it's obvious, life is a stupid repetition of clumsy mistakes). Conchita set off once more toward the rear of the house to refill the cups with steaming coffee.

She extended a cup to Carmela, then sat down and began to sip her own. She didn't dare raise her eyes to look at Carmela head-on. She felt a mixture of a fear and impatience. Carmela would be going through the same thing. How well they knew each other. It made her glad. So why was there any need to speak? Surely Carmela would be thinking the same way. But it was Conchita who said out loud (perhaps too loud) the idea that had been lancing her brain for a good long time. She exploded:

"We can't allow her to lose anything. Not the house, not the furniture, not the jewelry, not the clothes, not the money in the bank, not . . ."

"Not a pin," Carmela finished. It had all been said, thought Conchita with relief. Agustina could die at ease.

When Conchita got to the hospital that night to take care of Agustina, she was embarked on a singular mission. Agustina had just come out of the anesthesia and she was surrounded by plastic and metal. An IV dripped into her arm, and from her nose emerged some tubes that shocked Conchita. She would have preferred not to see Agustina like this, but who else would take charge of her? The three of them were practically alone in the world, and it was her duty. You couldn't depend on Carmela when it came to hospitals. She'd never managed to overcome her irresistible repugnance toward the ill. It was strange, because Carmela could stand all types of misfortunes except for those that stemmed from the human body. More than an hour went by, while Conchita remained seated next to Agustina's bed. She waited until the lights were put out, and as sometimes happens with arguments making use of an untruth, she felt that one pretext was not enough, and so she reeled off six more. Each one, when she spoke it aloud, gave her the impression of only showing off more clearly the falsity and weakness of the lie. Agustina met her gaze sharply through the shadows, and Conchita never knew whether she understood what it was all about or not. But she got what she wanted. Agustina nodded her head and Conchita combed through the table drawer. Inside a cloth bag (fashioned, of course, by Carmela) Conchita found the key to Agustina's house.

"Carmela wants to clean before you come back. The refrigerator needs defrosting. The humidity, shut up tight as a drum, think how everything must be growing mold. It needs to be aired out once in a while. Feed the cats. I've got to find you a robe and a pair of white socks. The key, absolutely essential."

Conchita never knew why she felt obligated to repeat her monologue once she had the sought-after key in her hand. After that, Agustina slept a good while (or so it seemed).

And sure enough. Between Carmela and Conchita they opened the wardrobes (Where would she keep the bank book? Ah, here it is, among the underwear), pulled the moldy leather armchairs onto the patio, dusted the porcelain figurines, watered the plants, and fed Agustina's four cats.

It was this afternoon of general cleaning that produced a find:

love letters carefully wrapped in cellophane and tied up with a ribbon. All were addressed to "Tina" (Carmela and Conchita looked at each other with suspicion: they had never known of such a nickname being applied to dry Agustina) and signed by a certain Walfredo, although sometimes there was only a "W" drawn with baroque flourishes, and in others the unknown sender dubbed himself "Your lover," nothing more. Conchita could not contain herself:

"What a phony baloney she is!"

The two women were stupefied. For years, their friend Agustina had kept them in the dark. Why this secret? From them, who had never hidden anything from her. Conchita felt devastated in her true spinsterhood. Carmela tasted a disagreeable sensation of having been swindled.

For the rest of the afternoon and that night, Conchita, vomiting, didn't feel up to going to the hospital. Carmela decided not to comment. In the morning, after a sleepless night, she made the decision to throw the packet of letters into the garbage along with the dinner scraps. In this way Walfredo vanished from their lives, and only thus could they feel relieved.

To give Conchita some peace, from then on Carmela took charge of all the decisions and also the hardest work. She dusted, mopped, and boiled, all with a species of rage. Conchita went at night to take care of Agustina and there reported on the progress of the cleaning (so that she wouldn't guess, the poor thing, already on the other side), the care of the cats, the purchasing of supplies in the store; but she was careful not to mention the discovery of the love letters.

For her part, Carmela assembled in cardboard boxes Agustina's dresses, her winter clothes, and some lengths of cloth that she'd taken to accumulating in recent years. At a glance she decided who, among those closest to her, were to be the inheritors (naturally, neither Conchita nor Carmela wanted anything for themselves, the point was that "nothing should be lost"). There weren't many sheets, and they were a bit battered too. Agustina never had known how to take care of bed linen properly, there was no alternative but to say so, even though she was dying, poor thing. There remained the problem of the shoes. This would take careful consideration; she had no notion of selling them (the point was not to enrich themselves by Agustina's death, God forbid). The ideal thing would be to make use of them for a charitable act.

So that's how things were when, on a first winter day (the north wind came without warning) Agustina returned to her house. The illness had advanced too far, and the doctors decided that further hospital stay was pointless. It was better for to her spend her last days in her own bed. Luckily for Carmela and Conchita, who had almost finished distributing all of her belongings, Agustina couldn't walk. After she was carried to the bed semiconscious and dressed with with care, there they sat, Conchita and Carmela, one on each side. They needed to put a very delicate matter to her. A long time passed in silence. Carmela couldn't stand it and left the room. She left Conchita alone with Agustina. She never knew exactly what they said, but in half an hour Conchita burst euphorically onto the porch:

"She agrees. She agrees to get married *in articulo mortis.*"

The brand-new fiance was Carmela's nephew, the good-for-nothing Alfonso. In truth Agustina was about thirty-five years his senior, but this was the least important. The most important was to save the bank account, the furniture, the house.

The ceremony was quick and efficient. In less than fifteen minutes Agustina passed from spinsterhood to matrimony, with barely a weak movement of her head and a trembling signature guided by the hand (also trembling) of Conchita.

Next came a sudden worsening of the disease. Alfonso the new-lywed gained the right to make certain determinations. To Car-mela's horror, his first step was to sell the monumental living room set (it was all carved wood). Conchita and Carmela put up a weak resistance, although pure logic indicated that Agustina was never going to emerge from her sickbed or her room. So wasn't it preferable to send those pieces on their way (they were so old, and stubborn Agustina had held onto them since the catastrophe of '32)? Nonetheless, Carmela couldn't avoid an expression of an-noyance (that jaw, manifest as a ship's keel): look at the turns life takes.

Agustina was having difficulty breathing on the day that Conchita decreed the distributions of the handbags and costume jewelry (she was quite surprised that no neighbors wanted to ac-cept anything). Meanwhile the husband decided to sell the dining set too (it was caoba wood), and since no one offered to buy the whole thing, he sold it piece by piece. What remained to be re-solved was the problem of the four cats. Better to sacrifice them than to have them suffer, Carmela said.

One morning, still gusty with north winds, the doctor pro-nounced sentence: it was time for Agustina to return to the hospi-tal. Carmela and Conchita looked at each other in fear. Carmela pulled her hair anxiously, but it was Conchita who finally spoke:

"But doctor, she'll know she's dying if she sees how empty the house is."

When she was being carried in the stretcher, Agustina suddenly regained lucidity, looked all around her, and grabbed Carmela hand in anguish.

"I must be going crazy," she said, "because I don't see the din-ing room set," she said.

"Calm down, Agustina, you're making this up."

Agustina started to cry.

"*Mi madre*, I must be in bad shape. I don't see any furniture in the living room either."

Carmela calmed her again.

"You're having visions," she said.

After they closed the doors of the ambulance in which Agustina left them for good (she died half an hour later), Carmela breathed a sigh of relief: she'd done her duty until the end. Someday it would be her turn, and then Conchita would know how to do things. She looked sharply at Conchita and knew that there wasn't any need to speak (they understood each other so well). But she felt a foolish, inexplicable terror, and she could make out the same fear in Conchita's expression, and a rebellion she'd never before seen in her eyes. Alfonso said the appropriate words:

"We are nothing," he uttered. "Dust to dust."

Carmela suddenly felt very lonely. She guessed that now, finally, Conchita would move.

Uva de Aragón was born in 1944 and has lived in the United States since 1959. She is assistant director of the Cuban Research Institute at Florida International University in Miami, and has published nine books of stories, poetry, literary criticism, and plays, some of them under the name Uva Clavijo. "I Just Can't Take It" comes from her story collection of the same name, published in Miami in 1989. Her story "Round Trip" has been published in English translation in *The Voice of the Turtle* (1997).

Translated by Cindy Schuster

I Just Can't Take It

I just can't take it anymore, the old man said to her, collapsing into the seat by her side, and he smiled at her sweetly, trying to undo his words with his expression, because he had just realized that he wasn't merely saying it; it was more than a casual remark or a simple unburdening. He looked tenderly at his wife in the bed, that dear old woman in her eighties, his lifelong companion of almost sixty years. How blue her eyes still are, they're all she has left. My God, she's light as a feather when I sit her up in the bed, how different from that woman who gave me so many hours of love, who was so independent and full of life . . . It's already time to give her her medicine, but why bother? It doesn't make any difference . . . no, it's better, let everything go on as usual, don't let her suspect anything, why make her suffer? Or should I? I really ought to tell her, find out if she agrees. And if she doesn't? There's no other way. I just can't take it.

He automatically picked up the bottle of medicine and the glass of water and drew near to the woman who accepted it with silent gratitude. He stroked her gray hair with infinite tenderness and saw that two tears were rolling slowly down her wrinkled face. Then he regretted the thought which only minutes before had been an irrevocable decision. And even more, he was horrified at himself, at the monstrous idea that had occurred to him. He was going to have to find a way, no matter what.

Perhaps if he were to lie down for a while and wait for the worst of the heat to pass, the sultry hours, as he had read God knows where, it wouldn't be so much of an effort for him to walk to the drugstore to get the medicine. And there was no reason he had to do the laundry today; he could do it tomorrow. The important thing was that there was still a can of soup and something else left to eat, and they could make it last until the check came tomorrow.

If the mailman comes early, I can go shopping before lunch; I feel like eating watermelon. What will I think of next? Half an hour ago I was convinced it was the last day of my life, I was planning how to put an end to these two useless existences, and this dear old woman, who can't move or speak, looks at me with her blue eyes and they fill with tears and here I am clinging to the hope of eating a slice of watermelon.

He must have dozed off because he felt a sudden jolt, as if it were too late for something, and, sure enough, when he looked out the small window overlooking the patio he saw that the shadows of dusk were already stealing the daylight. He checked his watch. My God, he said out loud, it's almost eight o'clock, how could I possibly have slept so long, the dear woman must be dying of hunger. She was moving her lips slightly as if she were smiling at him. Do you want soup or would you rather have soup, he asked her cheerfully. He clumsily opened the can with the electric opener that his grandchildren had given him for Christmas a dozen years ago and which had not been working well for some time now. He pushed aside the memories of the years before his son took his family to California. Even though they were already retired and older, they had still enjoyed life then.

He looked in the cupboard for the measuring cup and followed the instructions so that he would add the right amount of water to the soup. Maybe if they had gone to live in the same state as his son then, everything would be different now. But why should it be different? He stirred the soup slowly with the wooden spoon. His bones would still ache just as much every morning. Helen would be just as disabled. The social security check wouldn't be enough, just like here. But he'd have his son . . . his grandchildren. No, who did he think he was he kidding? The indifference of his family would hurt even more. He tested the soup with his index finger and found it lukewarm. He left it on the burner a few seconds more. It's not indifference. It's modern life. And Eddy's no youngster anymore. He'll be retiring soon himself. Nobody has time for old people . . . There shouldn't even be any old people. No old people allowed. Look, here comes your loving husband with the soup.

He sat down next to the bed and with infinite patience fed her the soup one spoonful at a time. She looked at him with her blue eyes, as if she were asking him something, and he smiled back, look what tasty chicken soup your husband cooked for you, and gave her another spoonful, but God help him, he couldn't look her in the eye.

It will only take me a few minutes. The drugstore is open until nine and it's better if I pick up your medicine now because in the morning it's very hot.

He descended the five steps slowly and went down the sidewalk toward the drugstore. Halfway down the block, from her balcony, Mrs. Porter greeted him and he nodded his head but didn't stop, as he usually did, to listen to his neighbor's invariable report on her arthritis. I've got enough troubles of my own. All you see in this neighborhood are old people. Look who's talking.

A strange weight pressed down on his chest. Tomorrow the check will come and I'll buy a slice of fresh, juicy melon. The social worker will come and change the sheets and give Helen a bath—and life has been reduced to this, waiting for a green check, the twice-weekly visit of a girl with a sweet smile, the occasional phone call from my son or one of our grandchildren. The rest? The rest is always the same. Always some kind of pain. Always a new ailment. Always so much effort to . . . to do what? To keep clean, to eat, to take care of Helen . . . to keep us both alive.

Smith, the medicine for Smith, please. This pharmacist is new. He doesn't know me. Why would he ask for my Medicare card? Look, young man, I've been a customer here for five years and every month I pick up my medicine and nobody's ever asked me for my card; you must have the number written down there or something.

All his pleas were in vain. He could see the little white bags with his wife's name on them and the little bottles inside and there was no way that this nasal monster with glasses would give them to him. Just wait until tomorrow when I talk to Humphries and tell him what happened; then this snot-nosed kid will get what's coming to him. Nothing. Nothing will happen to him. What do they care if I get mad? I can't go to another drugstore. And even if I could, it's not like I spend a lot of money. And anyway, one way or another, Helen and I will soon be dead.

But my God, what if I die first? I don't know why I think that. Things will happen when it's time for them to happen. At least tomorrow is Monday and the mailman will bring the check and I'll do the laundry and buy the groceries, and damn, what I wouldn't give for a slice of watermelon in this heat.

Back in his tiny apartment without the medicine, he got undressed slowly, placed his clothes carefully on the chair, and went over to his wife's bed to make sure she was asleep. Good night, old woman, he said, even though her eyes were closed. Finally he went to bed. Our father who art in heaven, why Lord? Why have you abandoned us? Hallowed be Thy name. Maybe I should call Eddy? Yes, I'll call Eddy and tell him the truth. Thy kingdom come. He dialed 1 (619) 533–8654 slowly. Thy will be done. *Riiing* . . . Out there it's six-thirty in the evening. *Riiing* . . . On Sunday. On earth as it is in heaven. Eddy? It's Pop. No, nothing's wrong. Your mother's the same. It's just that . . . you know . . . sometimes I get lonely . . . and . . . For Christmas? You'll come in December? But that's six months from now. Yes, I understand. No son, I'm fine. Of course. OK, take care. Yes, when you can. No problem. Our daily bread. Good-bye, son.

And the old man cried himself to sleep.

He woke up with that damn pain in his hip. But as soon as I take my aspirin and do my exercises it will go away. Then he remembered. He had to go to the drugstore before ten to pick up the medicine. In this infernal heat. Of course today was the first Monday of the month and the social worker would come and the mailman with the check and he would have his juicy and refreshing slice of watermelon.

When he returned from the drugstore he didn't think he had enough strength to climb the five steps. He was drenched in sweat. He couldn't put the laundry off another day. There were no clean shirts left. If Eddy would only send him six more he wouldn't have to do the wash so often. He should have told him that last night. Hot as it was in that Laundromat. Back then, he never used to suffer so much from the heat. Back then . . . back then everything was different.

When he cooled off and gave Helen her medicine with the last of the juice, he went down again and sat down on the steps. Who would come first, Miss Martínez or the mailman? My God, I can't take it anymore. Another day, another week, how much longer, and what for? Even memories don't matter anymore, and there's nothing to look forward to. Well, yes, I do look forward to something. Look how excited I get over something as simple as a slice of melon.

Good morning, Mr. Smith. Good morning, Ma'am. Getting some fresh air? No, I'm waiting for the social worker and the mailman. But, don't you remember it's a holiday, the 4th of July, Independence Day? Yes, yes it's true.

Charles Smith, eighty-eight years old, got up slowly, climbed the five steps that separated him from his apartment, opened the door, and took his wife's thin body in his arms. She opened her blue eyes and stared into his; he avoided her look. He took the elevator to the top floor. Then, breathing heavily, he climbed the stairs to the roof. Finally he looked at his wife. I just can't take it anymore, he said. And with Helen in his arms, he leapt from the fifth floor.

Adelaida Fernández de Juan, born in 1961, is a doctor living in Havana. "The Egyptians" comes from her first book of stories, *Dolly and Other African Stories* (1994), which deals with her experiences working in Zambia between 1988 and 1990.

Translated by Dick Cluster

The Egyptians

The Egyptians at the hospital were a likeable group, a bit similar to us not only physically, but also because they were quite cordial and would even say bad things about each other.

We met Habib first, then Tolva, Farish, and Solyman, each of whom worked in a different medical specialty.

They were the first victims of our fears. We trained ourselves by asking them loaded questions, figuring out how best to interpret their answers so as to discover the spying that they were surely engaged in, because they would try to penetrate us, to lead us astray, and so we had to be alert.

When Habib asked me for the first time what life was like in our country, it spurred a series of meetings which our brigade chief deemed very necessary, and which we held night after night when all the doctors got back to the house we shared.

There we discussed the Egyptians' every question, and what we would tell them, and who, and when. Although it would take a lot of work to see clearly what evil intentions hid behind every conversation, it was essential, our chief said, to analyze it all very well.

When, later on, the Egyptians asked me to give them my opinion of Varadero, and tell them whether Stevenson was still boxing, I couldn't put it off until the nocturnal meeting and had to say yes, it was a great beach, and no, Stevenson wasn't in the ring any more—even at the risk of earning myself a fight with the chief, which was exactly what happened, because that was what was meant by consorting with foreigners, he said.

The meetings were busy ones, and there wasn't time to define exactly who were the foreigners there—us or the Egyptians, or both groups, or neither. This was always considered a secondary question, and I never was clear about it myself.

Little by little, we formed ties with them: after all we were colleagues, healers, and we hung up our stethoscopes together for ten o'clock tea in the little meeting room downstairs. Habib always told us when the tea was brewing, and he ran around to the library, operating room, wards, and even the Isolation Unit for tuberculars, to be sure that no doctor, Egyptian or Cuban, would miss out.

That's how it began, the daily show that provided divine inspiration for our sacred meetings. For many reasons, you couldn't miss it. On the one hand we didn't understand their English very well, and when we finally deciphered what they were asking, half of us pretended not to in order give the other half time to consult with the chief (who truly hadn't understood anything) and to get the questions across to him in sign language so he could answer the way he thought best.

Meanwhile the Egyptians waited with Pharaonic patience, not comprehending why it took two or three cups of tea to find out whether it was easy to grow black beans or whether Cuban winters were very long.

We had the misfortune of losing Solyman, who died of a heart attack four months after our arrival. He never knew that his comments, too, were meticulously dissected by our brigade, and that we all lamented his loss: the hospital found itself without a dermatologist, the group of Egyptians was minus a fellow countryman, and we had to cope with a narrowing circle of possible spies.

Little by little, life got more difficult. Our adaptation, which was supposed to happen quickly, dawdled; the promised visitors and the necessary support didn't arrive; and, worst of all, there was no response to the reports so meticulously crafted every night, after every meeting, covering each Egyptian remark that we discussed.

Farish never stopped murmuring and thumbing his prayer beads, piece by piece, even when riding with Tolva who, two or three times every week, offered to carry some member of our brigade to town in his car and to shop for our food with the money we turned over to him as soon as we started getting it.

Then our nightly sessions grew quicker, because our gumshoe work was limited to checking out whether, in the trajectory to and from the stores, any suspicious word had been heard. But except for the inevitable questions—"Does this oil seem okay?" "You're buying potatoes instead of rice again?"—the surgeon who served as our driver appeared to be squeaky clean.

When I got sick and couldn't leave the house for almost a month, Habib and his wife appeared and I let them in despite having no witness who would be able to testify that they had only come to give me a floral bouquet. "The die is cast, the chief will have to understand that the sick can't refuse flowers," I said to reassure myself. Still and all, I didn't feel at ease until Tolva arrived at nightfall with half the brigade in his car. "Because it's silly for you all to go on walking through these downpours when I live so close to you," he explained.

It was appropriate, we all agreed, to space our meetings out more, because the Egyptians had not kept up with their questions about our country—even if this was just a change of tactics on their part.

When Farish invited us all to his house for a meal, we didn't know what to do with our well-honed powers, because Tolva and Habib were so happy that they tended to forget all about us, and we spent most of the night with them speaking Arabic and us speaking Spanish among ourselves. All of us were quite animated, and as each group expressed its own longing, everyone got louder and louder—us with "*Lágrimas Negras*" and them with "Take Me Back to Cairo"—so we made more of a racket than the group of Italians we'd seen in the Havana airport at our departure ten months before.

The last time we had a night meeting, our pens at the ready to scribe the report about the Egyptians, we debated whether it was really necessary to wait till Wednesday to go to town if the mail should already have arrived by now. It would be better to ask Tolva if he could drive us tomorrow. Or had Farish said that morning that he would collect our letters for us?

Those folks must have been the world's most likeable spies, and, above all, the subtlest.

Achy Obejas, born 1955, grew up in the United States and currently lives in Chicago where she is a columnist at the *Chicago Tribune*. She is the author of the short story collection *We Came All the Way from Cuba So You Could Dress Like This?* (1993) and the novel *Memory Mambo* (1996), and has published her poetry in various U.S. magazines. "We Came All the Way from Cuba So You Could Dress Like This?" was first published in English, in the collection of the same name; a Spanish version appeared in the Cuban anthology *Pillars of Salt* (1996).

We Came All the Way from Cuba So You Could Dress Like This?

for Nena

I'm wearing a green sweater. It's made of some synthetic material, and it's mine. I've been wearing it for two days straight and have no plans to take it off right now.

I'm ten years old. I just got off the boat—or rather, the ship. The actual boat didn't make it: we got picked up halfway from Havana to Miami by a gigantic oil freighter to which they then tied our boat. That's how our boat got smashed to smithereens, its wooden planks breaking off like toothpicks against the ship's big metal hull. Everybody talks about American ingenuity, so I'm not sure why somebody didn't anticipate that would happen. But they didn't. So the boat that brought me and my parents most of the way from Cuba is now just part of the debris that'll wash up on tourist beaches all over the Caribbean.

As I speak, my parents are being interrogated by an official from the office of Immigration and Naturalization Services. It's all a formality because this is 1963, and no Cuban claiming political asylum actually gets turned away. We're evidence that the revolution has failed the middle class and that communism is bad. My parents—my father's an accountant and my mother's a social worker—are living, breathing examples of the suffering Cubans have endured under the tyranny of Fidel Castro.

The immigration officer, a fat Hungarian lady with sparkly hazel eyes and a perpetual smile, asks my parents why they came over, and my father, whose face is bright red from spending two days floating in a little boat on the Atlantic Ocean while secretly terrified, points to me—I'm sitting on a couch across the room, more bored than exhausted—and says, We came for her, so she could have a future.

The immigration officer speaks a halting Spanish, and with it she tells my parents about fleeing the Communists in Hungary. She says they took everything from her family, including a large country estate, with forty-four acres and two lakes, that's now being used as a vocational training center. Can you imagine that, she says. There's an official presidential portrait of John F. Kennedy behind her, which will need to be replaced in a week or so.

I fold my arms in front of my chest and across the green sweater. Tonight the U.S. government will put us up in a noisy transient hotel. We'll be allowed to stay there at taxpayer expense for a couple of days until my godfather—who lives with his mistress somewhere in Miami—comes to get us.

Leaning against the wall at the processing center, I notice a volunteer for Catholic Charities who approaches me with gifts: oatmeal cookies, a plastic doll with blond hair and a blue dress, and a rosary made of white plastic beads. She smiles and talks to me in incomprehensible English, speaking unnaturally loud.

My mother, who's watching while sitting nervously next to my father as we're being processed, will later tell me she remembers this moment as something poignant and good.

All I hold onto is the feel of the doll—cool and hard—and the fact that the Catholic volunteer is trying to get me to exchange my green sweater for a little gray flannel gym jacket with a hood and an American flag logo. I wrap myself up tighter in the sweater, which at this point still smells of salt and Cuban dirt and my grandmother's house, and the Catholic volunteer just squeezes my shoulder and leaves, thinking, I'm sure, that I've been traumatized by the trip across the choppy waters. My mother smiles weakly at me from across the room.

I'm still clutching the doll, a thing I'll never play with but which I'll carry with me all my life, from apartment to apartment, one move after the other. Eventually, her little blond nylon hairs will fall off and, thirty years later, after I'm diagnosed with cancer, she'll sit atop my dresser, scarred and bald like a chemo patient.

Is life destiny or determination?

For all the blond boyfriends I will have, there will be only two yellow-haired lovers. One doesn't really count—a boy in a military academy who subscribes to Republican politics like my parents, and who will try, relatively unsuccessfully, to penetrate me on a south Florida beach. I will squirm away from underneath him, not because his penis hurts me but because the stubble on his face burns my cheek.

The other will be Martha, perceived by the whole lesbian community as a gold digger, but who will love me in spite of my poverty. She'll come to my one-room studio on Saturday mornings when her rich lover is still asleep and rip T-shirts off my shoulders, brutally and honestly.

One Saturday we'll forget to set the alarm to get her back home in time, and Martha will have to dress in a hurry, the smoky smell of my sex all over her face and her own underwear tangled up in her pants leg. When she gets home, her rich lover will notice the weird bulge at her calf and throw her out, forcing Martha to acknowledge that without a primary relationship for contrast, we can't go on.

It's too dangerous, she'll say, tossing her blond hair away from her face.

Years later, I'll visit Martha, now living seaside in Provincetown with her new lover, a Kennedy cousin still in the closet who has a love of dogs, and freckles sprinkled all over her cheeks.

At the processing center, the Catholic volunteer has found a young Colombian woman to talk to me. I don't know her name, but she's pretty and brown, and she speaks Spanish. She tells me she's not Catholic but that she'd like to offer me Christian comfort anyway. She smells of violet water.

She pulls a Bible from her big purse and asks me, Do you know this, and I say, I'm Catholic, and she says that, well, she was once Catholic, too, but then she was saved and became something else. She says everything will change for me in the United States, as it did for her.

Then she tells me about coming here with her father and how he got sick and died, and she was forced to do all sorts of work, including what she calls sinful work, and how the sinful work taught her so much about life, and then how she got saved. She says there's still a problem, an impulse, which she has to suppress by reading the Bible. She looks at me as if I know what she's talking about.

Across the room, my parents are still talking to the fat Hungarian lady, my father's head bent over the table as he fills out form after form.

Then the Catholic volunteer comes back and asks the Colombian girl something in English, and the girl reaches across me, pats my lap, and starts reading from her Spanish-language Bible: Your breasts are like two fawns, twins of a gazelle that feed upon the lilies. Until the day breathes and the shadows flee, I will hie me to the mountain of myrrh and the hill of frankincense. You are all fair, my love; there is no flaw in you.

Here's what my father dreams I will be in the United States of America: a lawyer, then a judge, in a system of law that is both serious and just. Not that he actually believes in democracy—in fact, he's openly suspicious of the popular will—but he longs for the power and prestige such a career would bring, and which he can't achieve on his own now that we're here, so he projects it all on me. He sees me in courtrooms and lecture halls, at libraries and in elegant restaurants, the object of envy and awe.

My father does not envision me in domestic scenes. He does not imagine me as a wife or mother because to do so would be to imagine someone else closer to me than he is, and he cannot endure that. He will never regret not being a grandfather; it was never part of his plan.

Here's what my mother dreams I will be in the United States of

America: the owner of many appliances and a rolling green lawn; mother of two mischievous children; the wife of a boyishly handsome North American man who drinks Pepsi for breakfast; a career woman with a well-paying position in local broadcasting.

My mother pictures me reading the news on TV at four and home at the dinner table by six. She does not propose that I will actually do the cooking, but rather that I'll oversee the undocumented Haitian woman my husband and I have hired for that purpose. She sees me as fulfilled, as she imagines she is.

All I ever think about are kisses, not the deep throaty kind but quick pecks all along my belly just before my lover and I dissolve into warm blankets and tangled sheets in a bed under an open window. I have no view of this scene from a distance, so I don't know if the window frames tall pine trees or tropical bushes permeated with skittering gray lizards.

It's hot and stuffy in the processing center, where I'm sitting under a light that buzzes and clicks. Everything smells of nicotine. I wipe the shine off my face with the sleeve of my sweater. Eventually, I take off the sweater and fold it over my arm.

My father, smoking cigarette after cigarette, mutters about communism and how the Dominican Republic is next and then, possibly, someplace in Central America.

My mother has disappeared to another floor in the building, where the Catholic volunteer insists that she look through boxes filled with clothes donated by generous North Americans. Later, my mother will tell us how the Catholic volunteer pointed to the little gray flannel gym jacket with the hood and the American flag logo, how she plucked a bow tie from a box, then a black synthetic teddy from another and laughed, embarrassed.

My mother will admit she was uncomfortable with the idea of

sifting through the boxes, sinking arm-deep into other people's sweat and excretions, but not that she was afraid of offending the Catholic volunteer and that she held her breath, smiled, and fished out a shirt for my father and a light blue cotton dress for me, which we'll never wear.

My parents escaped from Cuba because they did not want me to grow up in a communist state. They are anti-communists, especially my father.

It's because of this that when Martin Luther King, Jr., dies in 1968 and North American cities go up in flames, my father will gloat. King was a Communist, he will say; he studied in Moscow, everybody knows that.

I'll roll my eyes and say nothing. My mother will ask him to please finish his *café con leche* and wipe the milk moustache from the top of his lip.

Later, the morning after Bobby Kennedy's brains are shot all over a California hotel kitchen, my father will greet the news of his death by walking into our kitchen wearing a "Nixon's the One" button.

There's no stopping him now, my father will say; I know, because I was involved with the counterrevolution, and I know he's the one who's going to save us, he's the one who came up with the Bay of Pigs—which would have worked, all the experts agree, if he'd been elected instead of Kennedy, that coward.

My mother will vote for Richard Nixon in 1968, but in spite of his loud support my father will sit out the election, convinced there's no need to become a citizen of the United States (the usual prerequisite for voting) because Nixon will get us back to Cuba in no time, where my father's dormant citizenship will spring to life.

Later that summer, my father, who has resisted getting a television set (too cumbersome to be moved when we go back to Cuba, he will tell us), suddenly buys a huge Zenith color model to watch the Olympics broadcast from Mexico City.

I will sit on the floor, close enough to distinguish the different colored dots, while my father sits a few feet away in a La-z-boy chair and roots for the Cuban boxers, especially Teófilo Stevenson. Every time Stevenson wins one—whether against North Americans or East Germans or whomever—my father will jump up and shout.

Later, when the Cuban flag waves at us during the medal ceremony, and the Cuban national anthem comes through the TV's tinny speakers, my father will stand up in Miami and cover his heart with his palm just like Fidel, watching on his own TV in Havana.

When I get older, I'll tell my father a rumor I heard that Stevenson, for all his heroics, practiced his best boxing moves on his wife, and my father will look at me like I'm crazy and say, Yeah, well, he's a Communist, what did you expect, huh?

In the processing center, my father is visited by a Cuban man with a large camera bag and a steno notebook into which he's constantly scribbling. The man has green Coke-bottle glasses and chews on a pungent Cuban cigar as he nods at everything my father says.

My mother, holding a brown paper bag filled with our new (used) clothes, sits next to me on the couch under the buzzing and clicking lights. She asks me about the Colombian girl, and I tell her she read me parts of the Bible, which makes my mother shudder.

The man with the Coke-bottle glasses and cigar tells my father he's from Santiago de Cuba in Oriente province, near Fidel's hometown, where he claims nobody ever supported the revolution because they knew the real Fidel. Then he tells my father he knew his father, which makes my father very nervous.

The whole northern coast of Havana harbor is mined, my father says to the Cuban man as if to distract him. There are *milicianos* all over the beaches, he goes on; it was a miracle we got out, but we had to do it—for her, and he points my way again.

Then the man with the Coke-bottle glasses and cigar jumps up and pulls a giant camera out of his bag, covering my mother and me with a sudden explosion of light.

In 1971, I'll come home for Thanksgiving from Indiana University where I have a scholarship to study optometry. It'll be the first time in months I'll be without an antiwar demonstration to go to, a consciousness-raising group to attend, or a Gay Liberation meeting to lead.

Alaba'o, I almost didn't recognize you, my mother will say, pulling on the fringes of my suede jacket, promising to mend the holes in my floor-sweeping bell-bottom jeans. My green sweater will be somewhere in the closet of my bedroom in their house.

We left Cuba so you could dress like this? my father will ask over my mother's shoulder.

And for the first and only time in my life, I'll say, Look, you didn't come for me, you came for you; you came because all your rich clients were leaving, and you were going to wind up a cashier in your father's hardware store if you didn't leave, okay?

My father, who works in a bank now, will gasp—*¿Qué qué?*—and step back a bit. And my mother will say, Please, don't talk to your father like that.

And I'll say, It's a free country, I can do anything I want, re-member? Christ, he only left because Fidel beat him in that stupid swimming race when they were little.

And then my father will reach over my mother's thin shoulders, grab me by the red bandana around my neck, and throw me to the floor, where he'll kick me over and over until all I remember is my mother's voice pleading, Please stop, please, please, please stop.

We leave the processing center with the fat Hungarian lady, who drives a large Ford station wagon. My father sits in the front with her, and my mother and I sit in the back, although there is plenty of room for both of us in the front as well. The fat Hungarian lady is taking us to our hotel, where our room will have a kitchenette and a view of an alley from which a tall black transvestite plies her night trade.

Eventually, I'm drawn by the lights of the city, not just the neon streaming by the car windows but also the white globes on the street lamps, and I scamper to the back where I can watch the lights by myself. I close my eyes tight, then open them, loving the tracers and star bursts on my private screen.

Up in front, the fat Hungarian lady and my father are dis-cussing the United States' many betrayals, first of Eastern Europe after World War II, then of Cuba after the Bay of Pigs invasion.

My mother, whom I believe is as beautiful as any of the palm trees fluttering on the median strip as we drive by, leans her head against the car window, tired and bereft. She comes to when the fat Hungarian lady, in a fit of giggles, breaks from the road and into the parking lot of a supermarket so shrouded in light that I'm sure it's a flying saucer docked here in Miami.

We did this when we first came to America, the fat Hungarian lady says, leading us up to the supermarket. And it's something only people like us can appreciate.

My father bobs his head up and down and my mother follows, her feet scraping the ground as she drags me by the hand.

We walk through the front door and then a turnstile, and suddenly we are in the land of plenty—row upon row of cereal boxes, TV dinners, massive displays of fresh pineapple, crate after crate of oranges, shelves of insect repellent, and every kind of broom. The dairy section is jammed with cheese and chocolate milk.

There's a butcher shop in the back, and my father says, Oh my god, look, and points to a slab of bloody red ribs thick with meat. My god my god my god, he says, as if he's never seen such a thing, or as if we're on the verge of starvation.

Calm down, please, my mother says, but he's not listening, choking back tears and hanging off the fat Hungarian lady who's now walking him past the sausages and hot dogs, packaged bologna and chipped beef.

All around us people stare, but then my father says, We just arrived from Cuba, and there's so much here!

The fat Hungarian lady pats his shoulder and says to the gathering crowd, Yes, he came on a little boat with his whole family; look at his beautiful daughter who will now grow up well-fed and free.

I push up against my mother, who feels as smooth and thin as a palm leaf on Good Friday. My father beams at me, tears in his eyes. All the while, complete strangers congratulate him on his wisdom and courage, give him hugs and money, and welcome him to the United States.

There are things that can't be told.

Things like when we couldn't find an apartment, everyone's saying it was because landlords in Miami didn't rent to families with kids, but knowing, always, that it was more than that.

Things like my doing very poorly on an IQ test because I didn't speak English, and getting tossed into a special education track, where it took until high school before somebody realized I didn't belong there.

Things like a North American hairdresser's telling my mother she didn't do her kind of hair.

Like my father, finally realizing he wasn't going to go back to Cuba anytime soon, trying to hang himself with the light cord in the bathroom while my mother cleaned rooms at a nearby luxury hotel, but falling instead and breaking his arm.

Like accepting welfare checks, because there really was no other way.

Like knowing that giving money to exile groups often meant helping somebody buy a private yacht for Caribbean vacations, not for invading Cuba, but also knowing that refusing to donate only invited questions about our own patriotism.

And knowing that Nixon really wasn't the one, and wasn't doing anything, and wouldn't have done anything, even if he'd finished his second term, no matter what a good job the Cuban burglars might have done at the Watergate Hotel.

What if we'd stayed? What if we'd never left Cuba? What if we were there when the last of the counterrevolution was beaten, or when Mariel harbor leaked thousands of Cubans out of the island, or when the Pan-American Games came? What if we'd never left?

All my life, my father will say I would have been a young Communist, falling prey to the revolution's propaganda. According to him, I would have believed ice cream treats came from Fidel, that those hairless Russians were our friends, and that my duty as a revolutionary was to turn him in for his counterrevolutionary activities—which he will swear he'd never have given up if we'd stayed in Cuba.

My mother will shake her head but won't contradict him. She'll say the revolution uses people, and that I, too, would probably have been used, then betrayed, and that we'll never know, but maybe I would have wound up in jail whether I ever believed in the revolution or not, because I would have talked back to the wrong person, me and my big mouth.

I wonder, if we'd stayed then who, if anyone—if not Martha and the boy from the military academy—would have been my blond lovers, or any kind of lovers at all.

And what if we'd stayed, and there had been no revolution?

My parents will never say, as if somehow they know that their lives were meant to exist only in opposition.

I try to imagine who I would have been if Fidel had never come into Havana sitting triumphantly on top of that tank, but I can't. I can only think of variations of who I am, not who I might have been.

In college one day, I'll tell my mother on the phone that I want to go back to Cuba to see, to consider all these questions, and she'll pause, then say, What for? There's nothing there for you, we'll tell you whatever you need to know, don't you trust us?

Over my dead body, my father will say, listening in on the other line.

Years later, when I fly to Washington, D.C., and take a cab straight to the Cuban Interests Section to apply for a visa, a golden-skinned man with the dulled eyes of a bureaucrat will tell me that because I came to the U.S. too young to make the decision to leave for myself—that it was in fact my parents who made it for me—the Cuban government does not recognize my U.S. citizenship.

You need to renew your Cuban passport, he will say. Perhaps your parents have it, or a copy of your birth certificate, or maybe you have a relative or friend who could go through the records in Cuba for you.

I'll remember the passport among my mother's priceless papers, handwritten in blue ink, even the official parts. But when I ask my parents for it, my mother will say nothing, and my father will say, It's not here anymore, but in a bank box, where you'll never see it. Do you think I would let you betray us like that?

The boy from the military academy will say oh baby baby as he grinds his hips into me. And Martha and all the girls before and after her here in the United States will say ooohhh ooooohhhhh oooooooohhhhhhhhh as my fingers explore inside them.

But the first time I make love with a Cuban, a politically controversial exile writer of some repute, she will say, *Aaaaaayyyyyy-aaaaaayyyyaaaaay* and lift me by my hair from between her legs, strings of saliva like sea foam between my mouth and her shiny curls. Then she'll drop me onto her mouth where our tongues will poke each other like wily porpoises.

In one swift movement, she'll flip me on my back, pillows falling every which way from the bed, and kiss every part of me, between my breasts and under my arms, and she'll suck my fingertips, and the inside of my elbows. And when she rests her head on my belly, her ear listening not to my heartbeat but to the fluttering of palm trees, she'll sit up, place one hand on my throat, the other on my sex, and kiss me there, under my rib cage, around my navel, where I am softest and palest.

The next morning, listening to her breathing in my arms, I will wonder how this could have happened, and if it would have happened at all if we'd stayed in Cuba. And if so, if it would have been furtive or free, with or without the revolution. And how—knowing now how cataclysmic life really is—I might hold on to her for a little while longer.

When my father dies of a heart attack in 1990 (it will happen while he's driving, yelling at somebody, and the car will just sail over to the sidewalk and stop dead at the curb, where he'll fall to the seat and his arms will somehow fold over his chest, his hands set in prayer), I will come home to Florida from Chicago, where I'll be working as a photographer for the *Tribune*. I won't be taking pictures of murder scenes or politicians then but rather rock stars and local performance artists.

I'll be living in Uptown, in a huge house with a dry darkroom in one of the bedrooms, now converted and sealed black, where I cut up negatives and create photomontages that are exhibited at the Whitney Biennial and hailed by the critics as filled with yearning and hope.

When my father dies, I will feel sadness and a wish that certain things had been said, but I will not want more time with him. I will worry about my mother, just like all the relatives who predict she will die of heartbreak within months (she has diabetes and her vision is failing). But she will instead outlive both him and me.

I'll get to Miami Beach, where they've lived in a little coach house off Collins Avenue since their retirement, and find cousins and aunts helping my mother go through insurance papers and bank records, my father's will, his photographs and mementos: his university degree, a faded list of things to take back to Cuba (including Christmas lights), a jaundiced clipping from *Diario de las Américas* about our arrival which quotes my father as saying that Havana harbor is mined, and a photo of my mother and me, wide-eyed and thin, sitting on the couch in the processing center.

My father's funeral will be simple but well-attended, closed casket at my request, but with a moment reserved for those who want a last look. My mother will stay in the room while the box is pried open (I'll be in the lobby smoking a cigarette, a habit I despised in my father but which I'll pick up at his funeral) and tell me later she stared at the cross above the casket, never registering my father's talcumed and perfumed body beneath it.

I couldn't leave, it wouldn't have looked right, she'll say. But thank god I'm going blind.

Then a minister who we do not know will come and read from the Bible and my mother will reach around my waist and hold onto me as we listen to him say, When all these things come upon you, the blessing and the curse . . . and you call them to mind among all the nations where the Lord your God has driven you, and return to the Lord your God, you and your children, and obey his voice . . . with all your heart and with all your soul; then the Lord your God will return your fortunes, and have compassion upon you, and he will gather you again from all the peoples where the Lord your God has scattered you.

There will be a storm during my father's burial, which means it will end quickly. My mother and several relatives will go back to her house, where a TV will blare from the bedroom filled with bored teenage cousins, the women will talk about how to make *picadillo* with low-fat ground turkey instead of the traditional beef and ham, and the men will sit outside in the yard, drinking beer or small cups of Cuban coffee, and talk about my father's love of Cuba, and how unfortunate it is that he died just as Eastern Europe is breaking free, and Fidel is surely about to fall.

Three days later, after taking my mother to the movies and the mall, church and the local Social Security office, I'll be standing at the front gate with my bags, yelling at the cab driver that I'm coming, when my mother will ask me to wait a minute and run back into the house, emerging minutes later with a box for me that won't fit in any of my bags.

A few things, she'll say, a few things that belong to you that I've been meaning to give you for years and now, well, they're yours.

I'll shake the box, which will emit only a muffled sound, and thank her for whatever it is, hug her and kiss her and tell her I'll call her as soon as I get home. She'll put her chicken bone arms around my neck, kiss the skin there all the way to my shoulders, and get choked up, which will break my heart.

Sleepy and tired in the cab to the airport, I'll lean my head against the window and stare out at the lanky palm trees, their brown and green leaves waving good-bye to me through the still coming drizzle. Everything will be damp, and I'll be hot and stuffy, listening to car horns detonating on every side of me. I'll close my eyes, stare at the blackness, and try to imagine something of yearning and hope, but I'll fall asleep instead, waking only when the driver tells me we've arrived, and that he'll get my bags from the trunk, his hand outstretched for the tip as if it were a condition for the return of my things.

When I get home to Uptown I'll forget all about my mother's box until one day many months later when my memory's fuzzy enough to let me be curious. I'll break it open to find grade school report cards, family pictures of the three of us in Cuba, a love letter to her from my father (in which he talks about wanting to kiss the tender mole by her mouth), Xeroxes of my birth certificate, copies of our requests for political asylum, and my faded blue-ink Cuban passport (expiration date: June 1965), all wrapped up in my old green sweater.

When I call my mother—embarrassed about taking so long to unpack her box, overwhelmed by the treasures within it—her answering machine will pick up and, in a bilingual message, give out her beeper number in case of emergency.

A week after my father's death, my mother will buy a computer with a Braille keyboard and a speaker, start learning how to use it at the community center down the block, and be busy investing in mutual funds at a profit within six months.

But this is all a long way off, of course. Right now, we're in a small hotel room with a kitchenette that U.S. taxpayers have provided for us.

My mother, whose eyes are dark and sunken, sits at a little table eating one of the Royal Castle hamburgers the fat Hungarian lady bought for us. My father munches on another, napkins spread under his hands. Their heads are tilted toward the window which faces an alley. To the far south edge, it offers a view of Biscayne Boulevard and a magically colored thread of night traffic. The air is salty and familiar, the moon brilliant hanging in the sky.

I'm in bed, under sheets that feel heavy with humidity and the smell of cleaning agents. The plastic doll the Catholic volunteer gave me sits on my pillow.

Then my father reaches across the table to my mother and says, We made it, we really made it.

And my mother runs her fingers through his hair and nods, and they both start crying, quietly but heartily, holding and stroking each other as if they are all they have.

And then there's a noise—a screech out in the alley followed by what sounds like a hyena's laughter—and my father leaps up and looks out the window, then starts laughing, too.

Oh my god, come here, look at this, he beckons to my mother, who jumps up and goes to him, positioning herself right under the crook of his arm. Can you believe that, he says.

Only in America, echoes my mother.

And as I lie here wondering about the spectacle outside the window and the new world that awaits us on this and every night of the rest of our lives, even I know we've already come a long way. What none of us can measure yet is how much of the voyage is already behind us.

Ena Lucía Portela, born 1972, is a student of language and literature at the University of Havana. "The Urn and the Name (A Lighthearted Tale)," appeared in the Cuban anthology *The Last Shall Be First* (1993).

Translated by Cindy Schuster

The Urn and the Name
(A Lighthearted Tale)

... Latin, *merda;* Sardinian, Portuguese, Catalan, Provençal, Italian, *merda*; Surselvan, Vegliote, *miarda;* French, *merde;* Spanish ... The flaming sword of looking through someone on the *Rubber Soul* album finally expels Julio, fallen angel, from the paradise of *Romance Linguistics,* Lausberg, volume I. "If you can't beat 'em, join 'em!" means put down the book and start clapping to the beat of the music *(Tatarara, tará, tará!).* A paradigm of resignation on the outside, in the labyrinth of his mind the Beatles suck, this shit is garbage, fuck you, Tata.

the girl

turns off the tape recorder and almost chokes from laughter on her cigarette smoke. Stretched out on the bed next to Julio, The Specter, also known as René, interrupts in order to smile about the delightful pastime of contemplating every facet of that dressed mannequin that constitutes his body in the mirror. Perhaps he imagines the restoration of the lost connection between them (including the girl) and common sense. Something more seemly, in any case, than three tongues and a single pale, brimming face.

"What's up, philologist, are you crazy?"

Julio throws the question back at the girl ("What do you think?") while, in an exercise of prolonged inertia, he continues clapping like an erratic metronome. The Specter's smile dissolves into the black line of his mouth on his pale, brimming face.

"Enough already!" The metronome stops.

A palpable acknowledgment of motives and accidents circulates throughout the house. The memory of his last exiguous supper makes Julio, now beyond any need for vortex or symmetry, blink. He doubles over the pillow and buries his head in it.

"I love music. There isn't a song in the world I like better than that one. Nonetheless, Tata," and he stresses this, "you will certainly concur with me that . . ."

she concurs with nothing

With nothing, Julio, nothing since the day you caught her in the act with worn-out jeans and disheveled hair, behind the boltless bathroom door in the Evangelist church, trying to slit her wrists with a table knife. She told you her name, Thais, and that nobody loved her despite all her many efforts to love everybody. With such dirty clothes, such alcoholic breath, and her indigo-tinged lips—she was a blotch, a social disgrace. You took a fancy to a girl with no roof over her head, and no rules either, gruff and foul-mouthed enough to make a sailor's parrot blush, one of those who eats pizzeria scraps and goes to bed in the snow with the first guy she meets. You forgot that in your country, Julio, it doesn't snow.

The Specter picks the snot from his nose and sticks it on the mirror. Two beautiful green booggers: one over the reflection of Julio The Indifferent and the other over Tata How Disgusting. "Hopefully they'll stay put," he thinks and also about how much he'd like to paint Julio's Latin manuscripts and even *Romance Linguistics,* Lausberg, volume I, green. The only reason he doesn't is to avoid any possible attribution of anti-Semitic symbolism to the simple pleasure of colors (green and flesh), to avoid the *happening.* He lights a cigarette and Julio lights one too and counting the girl's there are three now and the windows shut. The ascending empire of smoke almost collides with the heights of the ceiling.

"Perhaps we could play," The Specter says to himself and announces the

m e n u

1. Shanghai: each player gets seven cards from the fortuneteller's deck; arranges them according to suits and numbers; a two gets two; a seven gets three; no wild card; the Ace of Diamonds is the Bomb, that is, it gets three; when he holds the last card the herald calls out "Shanghai!" and lays out the perfect hand; if it's not, he gets one. Today it's Julio's turn to win.

2. I Spy: "stamps fly": you see something in particular; say "I

Spy" (we can deal with the stamp question later); I indicate the color to prove that I've seen it with hints as to proximity and temperature. (This game, of course, has degenerated a lot. They used to say "hot," or "cold," but in the last round the girl had already begun to insist on "degrees of tepidity.") Even when it's not his turn, Julio always wins.

3. Garrofilation: "In the beginning was the Word and the Word was in God and the Word was God;" to penetrate the mystery of semantics and discover a meaning; which is equivalent to solving a system of equations in the variable "garrofilate" (e.g., Is it possible to garrofilate naked in the middle of the street?). The verb "to crackle" is prohibited.

Julio perks up at this proposal, the ultimate time-killing discourse, and puts the book away under his pillow. The girl elevates her spatial plane from the floor to the bed to declare her opposition because:

i'm hungry

and the philologist is a cheat, he hides cards in Shanghai, he says he put's them on the floor so he won't drop them, and he doesn't seem to be joking; his riddles for I Spy are composed of gray smoke and even grayer spider webs and, as if it were inconsequential, he says that the Word would be God, but that the beginning was an awfully long time ago and now the Word is nothing more than an alternative experience, a stupid garrofilation, and with this he initiates one of those interminable discussions of tropical philosophy during which, as you know only too well, René, we all lose patience . . .

"There's nothing we can do about your hunger, Tata," says Julio, "the fridge is empty and we've sealed up the door."

"Suffering the fate of Ugolini was a unanimous decision," says the Specter, "we can smoke, or sleep . . ."

Since you couldn't manage, Julio, to get her to tell you where she lived, you brought her home (the very home where you're all now rotting) and then you got the bright idea of a cup of hot chocolate and a blanket. In the middle of August. Thais, neither gruff nor foul-mouthed, admitted her scarce-practically-nil need for such courtesies, although of course, she thanked you very much for them, even though what she really wanted was permission to use the shower, a really cold shower so she could sober up.

rené

also known as The Specter, came two days later to stay. Diabolically (spectrally) thin, hunched over and dressed in black, on Mondays he always wants to be Yehudi Menuhin's first violin; on Tuesdays, Vyasa, author of *Mahabharata;* on Wednesdays, a dandelion; on Thursdays, a transvestite Greek wrestler, and only on weekends does he assume his true personality free from weeping and wailing. All at a very slow *tempo*—living one episode at a time, soap opera *tempo,* even when he declares, excited, that something is rotten in Denmark or when he mimics the voice of Laurie Anderson on the *Big Science* LP and comes up with his own answer to the question *What is behind the curtain?* (Polonius The Superstitious). He hasn't left the house for two weeks, obsessed with the idea that the street doesn't exist.

He injected us, Tata and me, with this idea, in session after session, until he finally convinced us to seal up the door. To stave off the abyss! And the son of a bitch is so sure of himself! (Immutable René). What began as an unraveling of old ways of thinking, an abolishing of beliefs, soon led to new ways of thinking and beliefs easily introduced into everyday life. And we're still hanging in there; when it occurs to us to question the stability of the ground we walk on (an earthquake-proof life) then we'll see what happens. For the moment, and perhaps indefinitely, I see no reason to worry: in reality (how hard it is for me to say that word!), street or no street, it's all the same.

Sometimes she gets nervous. After all, she's the youngest of the three. Julio remembers the plop-plop of dripping water, the tap-tap of the nasty little puddle-crushing plaster chips, and the simultaneous splashing to the inevitable parody of a Beatles' song through the absence of doors and curtains. In exchange for the epic in the Nordic winter, they offered him a pleasant sense of excitement. Dawn cracked on the clock between their glasses of tea with lemon. Julio listened to a girl tell her troubles. In love with some guy named Enrique Jordán, she had let him

beat her

horribly on a number of occasions, but she got fed up and left Enrique and left school (Math, unmistakable evidence of anal-retentiveness). Her Marxism professor had called her sullied and anti-aesthetic; sullied, fine, but no way was she anti-aesthetic, despite the F's that rained down on her in Algebra and Analysis.

This new dawn also cracks as the clock announces the corrosion of three stomachs by their gastric juices. The two booggers have hardened on the mirror ("I wonder if you could make little figures out of that stuff?" The Specter asks himself as he walks toward the bathroom), but the reflections had shifted some time ago.

three corroded

stomachs ("Imagine what they look like on the inside!" thinks
The Specter from the bathroom as he pulls down his pants) do not
necessarily guarantee the success of a heroic performance.

"Ugolino della Gherardesca," reads the girl from the ency-
clopedia, "tyrant of Pisa, of the Ghibelline party, [. . .] immortalized by Dante in his *Divine Comedy,*" how melodramatic . . .
do you guys think anyone will devote himself to immortalizing
us?"

Neither this language of the crypt nor the sounds and smells
emanating from the bathroom where The Specter defecates something vague with the door wide open manage to astonish Julio.

"Immortality, whether it's real or metaphorical," he declares,
"can be quite unpleasant, Tata."

The girl smiles.

"Hey René, stink-butt . . . want me to immortalize you?"

They hear a fart to which she attributes affirmative cadences.
But no camera appears and no flash goes off. (How fitting it
would be for The Specter to be immortalized absorbed in the
practice of what he considers to be the thirteenth art.)

why doesn't anybody

knock on the door? Where are the neighbors and the firemen and
the police? Could it be true that the street doesn't exist? Look,
Thais, relax, get it out of your system. It looks like these morons
are going to drive you to the insane asylum (Oooh, how scary!).
Listen, do what I tell you. Understand that you no longer care
how things begin or end; it's quite possible you're pregnant and
don't know by whom (please, don't even think about bringing an-

other little moron into the world). Julio told you that any girl who went with him ran the risk of returning with a Julio Jr., but he didn't specify if he meant a baby or a stunted adult; you can't even remember the last time you ate.

"Why doesn't anybody, why?" thinks the girl. "Who is Julio? Yes, like me, an *ex-fool on the hill*, Gaius Julius Verne Cortázar. Who is René? All right, yes, also an ex-actor from the theater with the door behind the stage. I've heard rumors that he almost strangled some playwright by the name of Vitia who demanded that he clean up the stage—full of sawdust, Styrofoam, and ochre and red paint—after a show. And me? Who am I? (Silly question.) My name is Thais of Alexandria, and at the moment I'm thinking up titles for personal confessions. If we run out of cigarettes I'm screwed."

The ex-actor from the theater with the door behind the stage comes out of the bathroom and throws himself on the bed again. The *ex-fool on the hill* reaches under the pillow for his book. The girl then proposes that they play at something else. They look at each other: the thought hadn't occurred to them. And there's so much to think about! Since there are not two but three of them (piece of a mystical quotient, to restate the obvious) a tiny factorial symbol (!) winks at them behind the "usual" number of positions.

(They almost always take so long to decide that in the end they're too tired to do anything but sleep.)

"I'm not in the mood," says The Specter, alarmed by the proximity of the interminable prelude.

The girl looks at Julio. The tiny factorial symbol (!) has disappeared and, at any rate, according to her, between two there's not much to discuss. The Specter wonders if this free version of Ugolino's fate might not in fact be too free.

It's not that it bothers me: I knew other penetrating and penetrable dimensions before Julio and Thais came along. It's a question of method. All right, look, let me see if I can explain.

the actor

has no reason "to be" the character. Moreover, there is no possible way he could be. The point is to realize the closest approximation, but, and this is important, it must be evident throughout the play that it's nothing more than an approximation. The balancing point between "to be" and "not to be" is different for everybody. Now do you understand? I'm pretty sure Ugolino and his sons wouldn't have spent their time doing what I'm looking at now, at least not while they were shut up in the tower. Cannibalism? Well, that's more of a possibility and there is a certain correspondence . . .

The Specter picks up the cigarette that has fallen from the girl's hand and observes the lovers, next to him in bed. He feels as if he were contemplating the copulation of two corroded stomachs. Julio bites the girl's nipples, and she insists on seeing herself like this in the mirror.

"I wouldn't recommend it," intervenes the Specter, "you two look pretty ridiculous."

A strange smile materializes on Julio's face, deformed by the pleasure which culminates when The Specter extinguishes the cigarette on his back and the smell of singed flesh fills the air. "If Tata decides to leave her clothes off," he thinks as he buttons his pants, "we'll be immortalized in a Manet."

Acknowledgments

My thanks to Jafet Enríquez and Mario Matamoros, who interchanged messages, greetings, hints, and other pressing matters between the two shores; to Arline García, invaluable collaborator; to Dick Cluster, both collaborator and meticulous translator; to Cindy Schuster, equally meticulous translator; to Nancy Alonso, who, when I get tired of looking for a misplaced piece of information, summons up the patience to find it; to other friends who have helped without knowing it; and finally to my mother, Nena, always looking out for me, until her last moment, to make things go as well as they possibly could.

Credits

"Women's Voices from the Great Blue River" was written for this volume by Mirta Yáñez. Translation copyright © 1998 by Dick Cluster and Cindy Schuster.

"My Aunt" by Esther Díaz Llanillo is a translation of "La tía." Rights reserved by the author. Translation copyright © 1998 by Cindy Schuster.

"Japanese Daisies" by María Elena Llana is a translation of "Margaritas japonesas." Rights reserved by the author. Translation copyright © 1998 by Cindy Schuster.

"A Whiff of Wild Desire" by Sonia Rivera-Valdés was originally published as "El olor del desenfreno." Rights reserved by the author. Translation copyright © 1998 by Dick Cluster.

"Catalina in the Afternoons" by Magaly Sánchez is a translation of "Catalina en las tardes." Rights reserved by the author. Translation copyright © 1998 by Cindy Schuster.

"I Just Can't Take It" by Uva de Aragón was originally published as "No puedo más." Rights reserved by the author. Translation copyright © 1998 by Cindy Schuster.